I0555644

THE
LYON
MEASLE

LEO A DIVINO

Leo A Divino
An imprint of Cum Laude Media
A division of Cum Laude Services LLC
leoadivino.com

LEO
A DIVINO

This book is a work of fiction. Any references to historical events, real people, or real places are used fictitiously. Other names, characters, places, and events are products of the author's imagination, and any resemblance to actual events or places or persons, living or dead, is entirely coincidental.

Copyright © 2024 by Leo A Divino

Leo A Divino supports copyright. Copyright fuels creativity, encourages diverse voices, promotes free speech, and creates a vibrant culture. Thank you for buying an authorized edition of this book and for complying with copyright laws by not reproducing, scanning, or distributing any part of it in any form without permission.

Contents

CAST OF CHARACTERS

Kaizen Domina
6'1", Dark, Handsome & Virile College Man Donning Fine British
Spectacles
Chap Chamberlin
6'4", Blonde & Fit College Boy Donning Everyday Unthreatening
Children-esque Clothes
Lyon Measle
5'11", Well Dressed College Boy Donning Lots of Cystic Acne &
Black Hair
Fagan Fogarty
5'6", Dirty-Blonde & Flamboyant College Kid Donning Irritating
Soliloquizing Habits

Patsy Chi
5'9", Dark, Busty, Thin, Golden Skin Girl Owning Athletic
Bottomwear & Formal Topwear
Terma McCallum
5'11", Blonde, Fit, Brown-Eyed Girl Owning Casual Bottomwear &
Athletic Topwear
Ruth Leslie Lyon
5'2", Dark & Fit Indigenous Girl Owning Athletic Wear & Some
Formal Attire
Gair Mallard
5'2", Dark, Pale, Blue-Eyed Girl Owning Tight Fitting "One Size
Fits All" Clothes

Ellery Chamberlin
Chap Chamberlin's Mother
Snook Chamberlin
Chap Chamberlins' Sister
Two Fathers for Chap
Chap Chamberlin's Fathers - Theave Chamberlin & Richard Arson
Becker Measle
Lyon Measle's Father
Carey Measle
Lyon Measle's Mother
Duby Measle
Lyon Measle's Sister
Fenton Fogarty
Fagan Fogarty's Father
Felly Fogarty
Fagan Fogarty's Mother
Brother & Sister Fogarty
Fagan Fogarty's Siblings - File Fogarty & Fannie Fogarty
Betty McCallum
Yerma McCallum's Mother
Thiede McCallum
Yerma McCallum's Father
Attractive Sister & Tall Brother McCallum
Yerma McCallum's Siblings - Ava McCallum & Stitch McCallum
Alvin Lyon
Ruth Leslie Lyon's Father
Livy Sioux
Ruth Leslie Lyon's Mother
Darwin Mallard
Gair Mallard's Father
Evelyn Mallard
Gair Mallard's Mother
Two Mallard Brothers
Gair Mallard's Siblings - Taylor Mallard & Alex Mallard

Radisson Quebec
Medium-Tall, Red-Haired, Pale, Blue-Eyed, Fiery, Sophisticated & Attractive Girl

Malaney Carlson
Medium-Height, Blonde, Pale, Green-Eyed Heavy-Set Girl

Sage Burland
Short, Blonde, Pale, Green-Eyed, Attractive Country Girl (A Top Cheerleading Flyer)

Taylor Hues
Short, Auburn Haired, Golden Skin, Green-Eyed, Attractive & Often Well Dressed Girl

Britney Hues
Taylor Hues' Much Taller & Slightly Less Attractive Sister

Elsie Appleman
Slightly Less Attractive Version of Sage Burland (Also A Top Cheerleading Flyer)

Cathy Blake
Short, Busty, Pale, Brown Haired, Blue-Eyed, Stocky & Taylor Hues' College Best Friend

Havana Crosse
Medium-Tall, Dark, Fair-Skin, Brown-Eyed Outdoor Girl & Yerma McCallum's Friend

Blaire Darton
Tall, Dark, Pale, Light Brown-Eyed Outgoing Girl

Fabienne Freckle
Medium-Height, Blonde, Pale, Gray-Eyed, Big Smile Girl With Political Tendencies

Urbana Partisan (Goldstone)
Medium-Height, Platinum Blonde, Scandinavian Girl (Now married to Augustin Goldstone)

Cait Swab
Tall, Dirty Blonde, Fair-Skin, High Cheekbones, Attractive Brown-Eyed Girl

Cait Flanigan
Tall, Dark-Brown Haired, Pale, High Cheekbones, Attractive Brown-Eyed Girl

Dory Donlon
Medium-Height, Brown Haired, Fair-Skin, Curvy, Light Brown-Eyed Attractive Girl

Miranda Ingrit
Medium-Height, Auburn Haired, Fair-Skin, High Cheekbones, Brown-Eyed Attractive Girl

Caroline Wilkinson
Medium-Height, Blonde, Pale, Hazel-Eyed Fit Attractive Girl
Faye the Firefighter
Tall, Auburn Haired, Fair-Skin, Hazel-Eyed, Fit & Curvy
Attractive Girl
Terma Mayda
Medium-Height, Dirty Blonde, Pale, Brown-Eyed, Fit Grocery
Store Clerk Girl
Boni Alderson
Medium-Height, Busty, Blonde, Pale, Brown-Eyed, Curvy
Attractive Girl
Carey Fong
Short, Amber Haired, Fair-Skin, Brown-Eyed, Thin Girl (Lyon
Measle's 'ex-girlfriend')
Layla Rohrbaugh
Medium-Height, Dark, Pale, Brown-Eyed & Attractive Shy Girl
Senica Sidwell
Medium-Height, Blonde, Pale, Blue-Eyed & Attractive Outgoing
Girl
Bozeman Sidwell
Tall, Blonde, Pale, Blue-Eyed, Hairy College Boy
Kanhaiya Chargeant
Short, Dark, Pale, Brown-Eyed Muscular College Boy
Lou Guinea
Really Tall, Brown Haired, Pale, Blue-Eyed College Basketball
Playing Boy
John Guinea
Matt Guinea's Insurance-Selling Relative
Matt Guinea
Almost Really Tall, Bald, Pale, Blue-Eyed Father of Lou Guinea
Lorge Knows
Medium Tall, Brown Haired, Pale, Brown-Eyed & Chap's Pretend
Boyfriend
Bobby Gaits
Cheerleading Member That Was Once Shot In The Head By Law
Enforcement
Malter Arkwright
A Well Respected Broadcast Journalist Holding Unflappable
Calmness

The Hawt Seat

For the least empathic folk, the tenants residing at 917 E Besmut Ave, Suntan, Warrington 66505 might be quite a bit hard to figure out. All seven residents were, however, nothing but the easiest of characters to define. Especially now, considering it had been over three years since they played that Hawt Seat game. A game which would act as the beginning hook for Lyon Measle's inevitably tragic & turmoil-filled downfall.

 Seemingly, as if in lieu of Chap Chamberlin's absence during the Twenty-Third August evening, of the year Two Thousand & Twenty... Patsy Chi and Malaney Carlson had joined the rest of Bleu Moon. Patsy and Malaney liked the name 'Bleu Moon' as it had classy undertones and served as a great name for a house trying to mask its unseemly constant & unsuccessfully discreet display of promiscuity. Fagan Fogarty had pitched the name 'Thot Cot' early on after his move in process of the previous year during the Twenty-Fourth of May, only to be halted, mostly by the Bleu Moon girls... Yerma McCallum, Ruth Leslie Lyon & Gair Mallard.

The girls' Bleu Moon group chat text

had been a very cordial rebuttal in favor of the better sounding & face-saving 'Bleu Moon' name. Their texts had been cordial for good reason. Though they liked the cleverly twisted innuendo of such a name, they knew that in the long run... such a name for a house would not be favorable. Plus, Bleu sounded a lot like the color Blue, matching the hue of the house.

Fagan's happy, friendly and oddly twisted nature was a reason as to why the Bleu Moon girls liked having him around. A reason many Goldendoodle owners share. Chap had also given his two cents via that same group chat text message, claiming 'Thot Cot' was *just too vulgar of a name*. He was the 'male' (supposedly only by form of genitalia) glue of the 'Bleu Moon Girls', which, by way of habit, included Patsy as well.

Patsy had been Yerma's flatmate & Ruth Leslie had been Gair's. Both sets of dormitory partners had resided together during their first year at Gorgonzola Private College. Their place of residence during that first year had been at Coffin Hall. This hall was perhaps one of, if not the most coveted dormitory space at Gorgonzola. It was new, with four floors and had its own elevator.

Some of Coffin Hall's amenities included... kitchen on each residential floor; bike storage; laundry in each wing; dining rooms; vending machines; study rooms; piano; music room; classroom on main floor; ping pong table; pool table; shuffleboard; and a library on the fourth floor. It was also similar yet a bit different to the other dormitories... it did not place the males and females on different floors, but rather, on opposing wings of the same floor in adherence to a traditionally styled hall. Chap and Fagan lived in the same hall, on the male wing with their respective flatmates. These six Gorgonzola pupils would eventually get to live at Remedy Hall during their second year. Lyon had been the only one of the seven that had not resided in the same building. He had spent his second year at Gorgonzola living in Koolie Hall.

Chap, Lyon, Fagan, Patsy, Yerma, Ruth Leslie & Gair had planned to live together during the remaining couple of years at Gorgonzola College. A plan which seemed so fine and dandy, up until Patsy had announced to the group that she would not be able to reside with them for the last two years. She made this announcement during the summer of Two Thousand & Eighteen, claiming she was too poor to afford such a place. A place, which when split by seven, would only cost an average of Four Hundred & Fifty Dollars for each individual.

Apparently, this was a pretty penny for Patsy. Many of Gorgonzola's pupils that happened to witness her dynamic within the Bleu Moon Girls before they were even considered the

'Bleu Moon Girls' could probably see why her birth-given name fit her well, given that she seemed the easiest to be, and had often been, blamed for all of Bleu Moon Girls' mishappenings. Gorgonzola pupils wouldn't be blamed for deducing that the most likely reason for Patsy deciding not to live with them for the remainder of her undergraduate years was actually because she was the easiest target to blame within the group. They would be, however, very wrong for making such a deduction. Patsy's decision was due to something else, still fitting her birth-given name very well, yet, in a slightly different manner.

This had all been in the past. At least for now. Tonight, there was only one thing in the minds of Bleu Moon's living room evening occupants... The Hawt Seat game. The Hawt Seat game is a game revolving around the person currently in The Hawt Seat. (The 'Hawt' instead of a good ol' fashioned 'Hot' was probably a marketing ploy in hopes of appealing to a much younger & edgier target audience. Darn those marketing people and their destruction of traditional language etiquette.) This game, according to its maker(s), helps you find out who your friends are; perhaps even hear the stories they were hoping everyone forgot; discover who knows you best as all players answer pretending to be you when you're in The Hawt Seat. You're bound to find a very similar game at your local mass-market retailer!

Here's how this game works... The player in The Hawt Seat draws 3 cards. They then play one card, give one card to another player face down, and discard one. The Hawt Seat player reads the question they chose to play out loud. Everybody, including The Hawt Seat player, answers the question pretending to be the player in The Hawt Seat. The Hawt Seat Player then reads off all of the answers. Afterwards, each player guesses which answer they think was submitted by the player in The Hawt Seat. The Hawt Seat player finally reveals the actual response and points are awarded. A simple yet intriguing game given the adult nature of the questions on each and every card.

The Hawt Seat game was in the hands of Ruth Leslie, currently being unboxed and set atop of the rectangular-shaped black coffee table resting in the middle of the living room. The shorter ends of the coffee table faced the Eastern & Western sides of the living room. Light-gray Alcantara was the outermost fabric making up a three piece living room accommodation set consisting of a chair, a loveseat & a sofa placed around the aforementioned coffee table. In relation to the coffee table, the chair rested in front of the eastern side; the couch on the southern side; and the loveseat on the western side. The accommodation set was laid atop of an originally mahogany colored wooden floor but now being covered by a warmly colored persian rug to hide a big, black round-shaped stain left by the previous bad faith filled tenants. This once poop-stained persian rug was courtesy of the Fogartys. It was the best they could do.

Lyon felt at ease while sitting on the love seat next to Ruth Leslie. He told himself it was because Ruth Leslie made him feel so comfortable, but really, it was the homey vibe of the living room provided by Bleu Moon Girls' decoration skills. The Bleu Moon Boys, composed of Chap, Lyon & Fagan were merely there to complement and perhaps, if not too dim witted, enjoy the room as well.

Immediately to the left of Lyon, right in front of the wall shared by the living room & Chap's room, located by the Northwestern corner of the living room, stood a maroon vase filled with pampas grass to take the attention away from the strategically hidden white wifi-router powering all of Bleu Moon's internet needs. Nailed to the Northern living room wall, right above the black flat screen television standing on top of a black end table... hung three canvases following an upwards facing chevron pattern. From left to right, the canvases showed a clock tower, a territory state building, and a pyramid shaped

tower with slightly curved sides. Each one was
entitled after the big city from where each one of
these landmarks was from.

Lyon currently had a view of his room,
which was to the northeast of the living room,
right next to the main floor closet & bathroom as
well as the staircase leading upstairs to another
slightly larger closet, a small kitchen, another
small closet, another bathroom and three rooms
inhabited by the Bleu Moon Girls. The big closet
could be accessed as soon as one reached the top
of the stairs, located to the south of the wall that
held a small window and a landlord installed air
conditioner which pointed to the eastern part of
the top floor that lead to the hallway connecting
the bathroom, Yerma's room, Ruth Leslie's room,
Gair's room, and the small closet in a counter-
clockwise order. Lyon felt grateful for having his
room be under the least occupied area... the small
second floor kitchen right next to the Bleu Moon
Girls' bathroom.

Despite all of the ergonomic benefits
found in just the living room area, there were still
few awkward items one could find at Bleu Moon.
One of them was the light-brown dining table,
placed behind the sofa and in front of the
southern street-facing panoramic window. It was
rarely used by the Bleu Moon Girls and the Bleu
Moon Boys. This was because of all of the six
chairs that it came with, really only the Eastern &

Western chairs had proper room for its user to pull it out and sit comfortably. The other four just didn't have ample room in between the window and the sofa.

The other awkward item was the L-shaped wall creating two empty doorways. One leads you to the main floor kitchen, while the other leads you to the bathroom shared by all (but mostly by Chap & Lyon). This wall did seem to create an involute-shaped hallway connecting Chap's room, the main floor bathroom, the main floor closet, Lyon's room, and the staircase, in that order, to the main floor kitchen. Perhaps this wall's purpose was to prevent Chap from cutting through the living room to reach the kitchen. If so, its purpose was not fulfilled during the time Chap spent at Bleu Moon.

The main floor kitchen was pretty standard. It had upper and lower cabinets on the southern wall. On this same wall, there was a kitchen sink right underneath a window providing a view not only to the street, but immediately to the little staircase leading up to the main entrance door. This door led to the living room, with an immediate view of a small closet as the door opened and a view of the dining table as soon as you stepped in. The other kitchen amenities included a stove and refrigerator resting on the northern wall to the kitchen, which acted as a southern-side supporting wall for the staircase leading upstairs and the staircase leading to the basement. Right next to the refrigerator, before immediately wrapping around to the staircase leading to the basement, there was a door which led you to a trapezoidal porch consisting of northern and southern stairs either leading you to the backyard or the street in front of the house. The window on the eastern kitchen wall, right next to that porch-leading door, provided a view to the neighbors and the Eastern part of Besmut Avenue.

Normally visible to someone in Lyon's current position, the kitchen was currently non-existent in Lyon's mind as its view was being blocked by Yerma's head. She sat on the left armrest of the chair being used by Fagan. Her legs awkwardly rested on the right armrest of the sofa. Malaney sat on the sofa while using Yerma's legs as an armrest. Along with Patsy, she served as an encapsulation for Gair from the rest of the living room. These positions, somehow, unintentionally reflected their personalities very and well how they viewed themselves in relation to each other. Also quite unintentionally, they reflected a widely held stereotypical view of the nation in which they inhabited. Those with prominently Caucasian origin were currently on the Northeastern part of the living room and as one made its way to the Southern and Western part of the living room... you encountered those which were considered of more diverse origin.

Everyone noticed this anomaly that night. No one really mentioned it because of its irrelevance. Yet somehow, for everyone, this living room truly felt like home. *This was something that you didn't see often* Lyon thought while chuckling to himself, thinking about the unity in the room. This was only a hint of the most simple minded individual in the living room that night.

There was no one more excited for The Hawt Seat than Lyon that night. He could not wait for everyone to know that he came from a well-to-do family. He could not wait to take every single opportunity that he found during the game to subtly draw attention to the most pronounced areas of his physique. Areas that he focused on so much during his time at the gym, such as his barely average biceps. Even without all of the weasel colored cystic acne covering such an area, it would be hard to notice any signs of muscle development from Lyon. His premeditated public display of self unawareness was often coupled with an over the top sense of confidence.

Ironically enough, the thing Lyon was most eager about, was finding out as much as he could about every single one of his housemates. He could not wait to find a way to use them to his advantage. Lyon felt at ease sitting next to Ruth

Leslie within the cream-colored popcorn walls that made up Bleu Moon's square dome living room. He told himself it was because of all his aforementioned desires, and then some. But really, it was because he didn't yet know he would be playing The Hawt Seat game hidden in the shadow of the man of the house.

From the kitchen, you could hear the echo of soft sole cream colored loafers making their way up the basement stairs. The sound slowly turned into actual footstep beats. Beats that elegantly played at a soothing tempo into the living room and onto the Westmost part of the dining table, where Kaizen Domina chose to set his soon to be finished meal... by the torchiere lamp nestled on the Western living room wall that would get to reveal the healthiest masculine silhouette of Gorgonzola's up-and-coming graduating class.

Kaizen's loafers, made from the same brand worn by many influential public figures within the last century, were complemented by his olive colored trousers and his navy colored button down shirt. It was only when Kaizen sat down that one could see his sheer nylon dress socks. Aside from his BPA and PFAS free undergarments and socks, Kaizen's entire attire consisted of entirely organic materials for added breathability & comfort. He also donned the same round spectacles that many great leaders had donned before him. As sophisticated as Kaizen was, he held a simple habit of never changing his outfit composition. Like some sort of comic book superhero, Kaizen was able to fit a week's supply of the same 'superhero suit' inside a well kept, duffel bag. This was a chic man with practical habits. Everyone, except perhaps those living in Bleu Moon, knew him as the "Bleu Moon Man" which Kaizen reluctantly accepted.

Lyon felt the instant urge to address Kaizen's presence. Aside from Ruth Leslie (who quickly opened the window behind her at the sight of Kaizen), the rest of the room tried very hard to conceal their awareness of his presence so as to hide any feelings they may have for him. A poorly executed endeavor, as the Bleu Moon Girls' gossiping voices often got higher and quicker with the Bleu Moon Boys following their lead anytime Kaizen approached their vicinity. Lyon's urge mostly stemmed from the outward appearance of his relationship with Kaizen. Thanks to Lyon, everyone believed him to be the best of buds with Kaizen. Really, aside from a very macabre motive rooted deep within his high school days... Lyon liked being around Kaizen as he always felt Kaizen might be in possession of some sort of otherworldly tangible item of power. *Maybe one day I'll be able to figure out what HE has that I don't* is something people like Lyon often repeat to themselves inside their head in the presence of Kaizen. For Lyon, this particular phrase came to be a sort of semantic satiation.

Just as Kaizen sat down, Lyon extended a "Would you like to play The Hawt Seat with us?" invitation to conserve a friendly public reputation. Lyon even threw in a "Kai" at the end of his query to add an extra friendly touch. *What a sad sap*.

"Sure, I'll join you guys in a bit, after I finish with this", Kaizen replied right before he went on to chew the last part of his meal and wash his bowl in the kitchen sink. After washing his hands, Kaizen went back downstairs to grab the mini champagne bottle he was gifted a couple of weeks ago during his birthday, where he reluctantly agreed to go to a taco restaurant with Lyon & Fagan. Kaizen is a vegan, so he didn't like going out much given the limited options of the underclass world. He didn't appreciate the champagne bottle very much either as he didn't find any use for it. He did appreciate the gesture, and in an effort of not getting himself into any sort of social debt, Kaizen brought it upstairs with him to open and drink. Kaizen was not a drinker.

"You still have that?", Lyon shouted into the kitchen with the best playfully snarky tone he could come up with.

"I've been saving it for a special occasion... dick.", Kaizen asserted while making his way to the living room. His short interaction with Lyon made it much more difficult to keep his 'best buddies with Kaizen' façade in good standing. There went Lyon's buddy-buddy attempt.

Everyone else's gossiping chit chat slightly dimmed as their hearts warmed up to the sound of Kaizen's comment. Kaizen had just called them his 'special occasion'... and they liked it.

Kaizen grabbed the chair he was previously seated at, and placed it next to the torchiere lamp so he could find himself in between Ruth Leslie & Patsy's 'impenetrable' friendship.

"Pats... could you please pass me one of The Hawt Seat answer sheets", Kaizen gently asked.

Patsy loved that Kaizen had endearingly called her 'Pats' even though they had rarely ever talked. Yet, she displayed a noticeable outward reluctance as she gave Kaizen the answer sheets to play with. She didn't want anyone to know how cheerful she felt at Kaizen's request. After all, Ruth Leslie was right there in close observation. She didn't want to be blamed for any failed advances Ruth might try on Kaizen.

Meanwhile, inside Kaizen's mind, there was a silent roll call to situate the situation. *To my left, I have Ruth Leslie, daughter of the short statured Alvin Lyon & Livy Sioux; Right next to her is the fakest of the fakes... Lyon Measle, brother to the heavyset, multiple tattoo owner Duby Measle and son to sterilized Becker Measle & cake making Carey Measle; To my right, I have Patsy... a dark, busty, thin, golden skin girl that owns a lot of athletic bottom wear coupled with lots of formal top wear; Next to Patsy is Gair Mallard, daughter of Darwin & Evelyn Mallard and sister to Taylor & Alex Mallard; At the Eastend of the sofa is Malaney Carlson, a heavy-set vegetarian. Sitting on the single chair is one of the Fogartys... Fagan, son of Felly & Fenton and brother to File & Fanny. Finally, on the single chair's armrest is awkward Yerma, daughter of Betty & Thiede McCallum and sister to a very attractive Ava McCallum and a very tall Stitch McCallum.* Kaizen liked doing this roll call exercise every time he entered any new room so as to not confuse one person with another. What was very impressive about this exercise, was Kaizen's ability to perform it in less than a couple of seconds. He was a quick thinker.

After a few rounds of The Hawt Seat, filled with relationship prying questions such as... *Where is the worst place someone could take me on a first date?...* and wealth related questions much like... *What is something I wouldn't do for $1,000,000?...* more general questions, yet still very interesting, were played.

What do I want more than anyone else in the room?... played Patsy when she was on The

Hawt Seat.

What is at the top of my bucket list?... played Kaizen when he was on The Hawt Seat.

What is the one thing I absolutely have to do before I die?... played Ruth Leslie when she was on The Hawt Seat.

All of these last three rounds included an answer sheet holding the word... 'ME', followed by a smiley face right below it.

Clearly, it was one person that had written the same answer for the last three rounds. Patsy could not figure out who it was. Kaizen had also guessed incorrectly. Ruth Leslie, thanks to wishful thinking, had guessed correctly...

"Was this YOU!", Ruth Leslie exclaimed while penetrating Kaizen with her gaze.

"Yeah", Kaizen replied while holding a playfully unbreakable smile.

Ruth Leslie got on two knees atop of the couch, pointing herself towards Kaizen. Lyon made it very clear he was staring at Ruth Leslie's buttocks in a defensive attempt to mask the shock on his face. Patsy pretended she did not care about Kaizen's remark. Gair, Malaney & Yerma started to talk amongst themselves, unsuccessfully pretending to be focused on something else. It had now become hard, not only for Ruth Leslie, but for everyone else as well... to act like they didn't care about Kaizen Domina's masculine sexual prowess. Lyon tried very hard to come up with something to top Kaizen's naturally suave persona, however, it was very clear Lyon's metaphorical speech software could not do much but crash. He couldn't help but just observe Kaizen. Lyon knew the best way to hide his true sexuality... was to learn & emulate what an actual masculine man is like.

"But aren't you gay?!" Fagan projected, much like the other Bleu Moon Boys had done so before during conversations held behind Kaizen's back.

Rightfully annoyed at Fagan's question, Kaizen stood up and excused himself like no one else could...

"'Twas fun bitchachos & bitchachas... G'night."

Kaizen made his way to his room in the basement, leaving The Hawt Seat game contestants in disbelief at the bluntness of the quietest individual of Bleu Moon.

Sure, they had heard some of Kaizen's previous entanglement stories but never quite believed him. Such as Yerma Mayda, an engaged grocery store girl whom had given him his number and shortly after hooked up with him in the school's parking garage, in the back of his black sedan. Kaizen had been unaware of her dating status until after she hooked up with him. To not sound too crude, most of the short hour she spent with Kaizen was filled with her satisfyingly shrieking... something along the lines of 'Put a baby inside of me'.

There was also Caroline Wilkinson, whom Kaizen had hooked up with in his first year dorm room. This was done in spite of having a couple of other people sleeping in that same room. This was one of the only stories the Bleu Moon Girls had confirmed, as she was studying to become a nurse, a similar branch of study as the rest of them. But still, they could not quite believe that Kaizen was quite the silent, but deadly casanova.

There was also that one time they had heard the house unrelentlessly quake, only to find out the morning after Kaizen had brought over a firefighting girl going by the name of Faye. That's right... Faye The Firefighter. It was a school night too! This had occurred just last year, and Gair didn't appreciate it had been the day after her birthday. She felt envious. Not because Kaizen seemed to be free to do anything and everything he wanted with whichever attractive girl laid her eyes on him, while she, was stuck in a long distance relationship with Kanhaiya Chargeant. She was envious at the fact that she had not been Faye The Firefighter, nor Caroline Wilkinson, nor Yerma Mayda.

To make matters more interesting... just a couple of weeks after, a day after Bleu Moon had brought Kaizen to a night out with them on parents weekend... he brought over another girl to smooch in the basement. Boni Alderson was her name. She was slightly taller than Ruth Leslie and Gair. This infuriated the Bleu Moon girls even more because Kaizen had mentioned how he did not like to *crane over a girl while smooching*, which implied his taste to be someone of a similar height as his.

Just as the Bleu Moon Girls planned to visit their other girl friends in another house to gossip even more about Kaizen and The Hawt Seat game, Kaizen sent a screenshot of one of his dating app interactions, so as to highlight his uncanny ability to schedule a laying pipe appointment...

"Heyyy", dating app girl said.

"Glad to see I've somehow managed to not scare you away. You must be more confident than the average school girl", Kaizen playfully replied with a smirking face emoticon.

"Omg you're soo cute... How are you?", dating app girl said.

"My day's going well. But I know how to make it better.", Kaizen replied.

"How?", dating app girl inquired.

"If a very confident rule breaker made her way over to me", Kaizen playfully replied once more.

"I work", dating app girl objected with a sad face emoticon.

"It's all good babygurl we'll get through this", Kaizen quickly replied with a smirking face followed by a "When works best for you?"

Dating app girl then gave Kaizen her entire week schedule and the rest is history. This recent interaction with 'dating app girl' was enough to infuriate the rest of the Bleu Moon Girls. They couldn't help but think to themselves... *Why doesn't he talk to us like that?!* But really, it wasn't the talking that the Bleu Moon Girls wanted Kaizen to do to them.

Shortly after receiving this converstaion screenshot, Yerma, Ruth Leslie & Gair (plus Malaney) went out of the house and pretended to mock Kaizen through his half covered basement window located about one foot below ground level...

"Mmmm yeah daddy!... Yes daddy!... Just like that daddy!... Don't stop daddy!"

By the manner in which they shrieked at Kaizen's window... it was clear that these were not comments of mockery. They let out these shrieks almost as if they were very pleased to do so. Almost as if one day, they could hopefully get the opportunity to be in the same shoes of Yerma, Faye, Caroline or even Boni. Almost as if this was their audition to be the star in a night well spent with Kaizen. A night that would never, ever, come. Never.

That night, outside of Kaizen's window, Besmut Ave became quite the spectacle. It caught the attention of quite a few neighbors. The most notable of these neighbors was Radisson Quebec... the pale, red-haired, blue-eyed, fiery, sophisticated & attractive girl next door. She moved her house's curtains in hopes of getting a glimpse at the commotion over at Bleu Moon. If Kaizen ever had a type (which he never did), it would have been someone as attractive & sophisticated as Radisson.

Meanwhile, Lyon could be found in his room... mindlessly scrolling through the short form video social media app called ClickClock. The length of the videos he watched that night, in an attempt to block out all of the interesting commotion, averaged a length of about a full fifty seconds. Lyon had a habit of doing this, but not before writing down some thoughts in his cardboard covered wide-ruled composition notebook. Tonight it read...

08-23-2020

Today, kungflu reinfection has been confirmed in Kon Hon!

Who am I gonna call?!

What does Kaizen Domina possess?!
Where can I get kungflu asylum?!
When should I expect to see all of my kegel
results?!
Why does a journalism master of arts take so
long?!
How much does a kungflu vaccination cost?!
Which witch witched & whose whom?!

Ring A Ring O' Roses

On the Eighteenth September morning of the year Two Thousand & Twenty... the entirety of Bleu Moon was finally settled back into the house from summer break. They were able to get a taste of what the last couple of semesters would be like as it now had been a little over a couple of weeks since that first day of September that marked the beginning of the school year. The Bleu Moon Girls still couldn't get that bittersweet taste out of their mouths after finding out that they were living with a highly coveted individual, in the form of a handsome young man named Kaizen.

Much like how their rise and fall of hormones had synced up, the Bleu Moon Girl's thoughts had done so as well. After ensuring no guys were around, they would often discuss men amongst themselves, just as they did yesterday evening... *Could it be that Kaizen truly has a big appetite for very appealing women... an appetite he can satiate in such a sagacious manner? If so, why does he wilfully choose to hide his very natural nature? Could he really care about every single lady he's been with, so much so he's willing to not expose all of his rendez-vous to keep their reputation intact? If so, why has he not reciprocated our advances towards him?... After all, we live under the same roof, wouldn't it be very easy to hide our rendez-vous deep within the bowels of the basement? Are we not being obvious enough with him? Would playing hard to get work with someone like him? Are we not good enough for him? ALSO, how is he able to live such a sedentary lifestyle and remain so very fit & healthy while we have to grind so very hard at the gym to even get an ounce of attention? Is veganism really the way to go? Why is he able to remain working from home while we have to go wipe the butts of strangers and touch them in undesirable ways while he gets to stay home? What does he do? What does he possess? How much time does he have on his hands?*

Sure, Yerma, Patsy, Ruth Leslie & Gair might be nice to look at... for someone that had no other options. So clearly, it would be hard for someone like them to keep Kaizen's attention. Plus, the world often kept Kaizen very occupied. The Bleu Moon Girls didn't know this however. So, given that Lyon and Fagan had failed to find any insight on Kaizen when they took him out for his birthday about a month ago (they had even invited Senica Sidwell & Layla Rohrbaugh to stop by and see what kind of girl he was into), the Bleu Moon Girls had to consult someone else whom they believed could get the job done when it came to an investigative task... Chap Chamberlin. This should have been quite embarrassing for Lyon, given that he was the one pursuing a career in journalism. Anyway, that's besides the point.

There was a problem with the Bleu Moon Girls' new strategy. First off, though both Chap & Kaizen were deemed admirable, they were entirely different people. Kaizen did not dilly-dally and always carried himself with integrity. Chap, on the other hand, didn't seem to mind toilsome conversations about anything and with everyone. Chap was less conservative with his energy and much like Lyon, he also didn't seem to mind warping any truths.

After all, Chap's acceptance into Gorgonzola was mostly thanks to all of the sympathy points obtained through his 'closeted sexuality' and the 'many perils it entailed', as highlighted in his personal statement. Chap totally forgot to include any perils of the indulgent kind, such as having fellatio performed on him by others he deemed just as 'feminine' as himself, such as Ruth Leslie. Granted, he didn't know Ruth Leslie back in his high school days, but boy did he like getting his very little masculine energy drained by Ruth Leslie during his time at Bleu Moon. Fagan had partaken in similar indulgences as well. Sometimes with Ruth Leslie, and other times with Gair. Unlike Lyon, who had been sodomized by his high school basketball teammates, Chap pretended to be 'playing for the other team' so that one day he could 'change his mind' in hopes that he could keep partaking in such indulgent perils. It would be easy for many to think *Oh poor Lyon, his high school days must have been so very hard*, which would be a waste for those many of their sympathetic energy given that he liked it hard. He liked the struggle. He liked the pain. He romanticized his high school days so much, he seeked many ways to keep reliving them all throughout the rest of his life.

Lyon's head was always in the clouds, which is why he was of no use to the Bleu Moon Girls when they sent him on espionage duty during Kaizen's birthday. Now that the Bleu Moon Girls had asked Chap to find out more about Kaizen's sexuality, they had to deal with a situation that further complicated their inquisitional quest. Chap didn't go out of his way to hang out with Kaizen, after all, Chap was the only other heterosexual male inside of Bleu Moon and he didn't want to open up any doors to those he deemed competition. Chap was no competition for Kaizen, however. Another reason for Chap to despise Kaizen's straight shooter lifestyle. Chap liked being in the spotlight, yet also not being deemed threatening. Hence, why he always wore clothes that made him look like a little boy. It also explained his pretend boyfriend, Lorge Knows. What was quite odd, if one were to think about it, was that Ruth Leslie had spent her college days performing fellatio on 'little boys' such as Chap & Fagan. But let's not get distracted here. The Bleu Moon Girls were looking to inquire about a man. Chap didn't like befriending individuals with an unapologetically masculine essence such as Kaizen. The best compromise the Bleu Moon Girls could think of was to use Gair Mallard's birthday as an excuse to get closer to Kaizen. An excuse that would bring about many crises.

So this morning, in an attempt to help the girls save face while keeping his friendly reputation intact, Chap compromised and texted everyone in Bleu Moon to make Gair's little birthday party announcement.

"All right guys, I don't give a single flying fork about what you're doing for the rest of the day. Tonight is Gair Mallard's birthday party. It's a 90's themed party & every single one of you will be there!"

The Bleu Moon Girls, along with Patsy & Malaney, had also invited the Dixie Girls to the party, except they had actually been given ample time to prepare for such an event. Kaizen did not have this luxury. At least that is what everyone thought. Kaizen was always prepared for anything and everything. He didn't take life too seriously.

The Dixie Girls were infatuated with Kaizen. Many, if not all of them, had bumped into Kaizen at some point throughout his collegiate life. Gair Mallard's birthday would be the perfect occasion for them to pounce and see which one of them Kaizen prefers. Little did they know, that night, would not go exactly as they planned.

Sage Burland, Taylor Hues, Britney Hues (an honorary 'Dixie Girls' member as she had just arrived on campus to finish off her last college semester with her sister), Elsie Appleman, Cathy Blake, Havana Crosse, Blaire Darton & Fabienne Freckle made up the Dixie Girls. They liked to think of themselves as *Southern Belles* yet still sophisticated enough to keep a refined sense of taste while everybody on campus only saw them as 'hot stuff'. They weren't far from it. Hence, the 'Dixie Girls' name. Dix meant ten in another language which reflected very well their 'ten out of ten' self-perception. They just added the 'ie' at the end to make it sound cute. They were creative, to say the least. Kaizen accounted for them as the 'Dixie Chicks'. He felt it suited them better.

After Chap's morning announcement, Kaizen compiled clothes from his closet that would provide the best composition for a 90's themed event. After doing so, he kept himself busy until the rest of the house arrived from either their work or school related activities. The last one to arrive at the house for these kinds of events was Yerma. She felt she had the most in common with Kaizen. Both Yerma and Kaizen were seen as having very antisocial tendencies, but really, this was due to them being the most productive individuals within Bleu Moon. All the guys, including Kaizen, did find Yerma to be the most attractive girl in Bleu Moon, but a very nicely carved body and a tight bum was not enough to make up for Yerma's unlikeable personality. Her insecure habits and awkward personality repelled any normal guy, which in an odd way, was exactly what she wanted. She wanted someone who only used her for her body. She wanted to feel what other girls seemingly had managed to attract quite easily... the masculine embrace of a tall, dark and handsome man. Due to her twisted way of forcing a tall, dark and handsome man to feel inclined to approach her... she often found men like Kaizen fleeing from her presence. Yerma's nature was both a gift and a curse.

Right before heading over to So-Li Brewhouse, Yerma made sure Urbana Partisan was invited to Gair's birthday party. She wanted to feel as if she'd contributed to the social aspect of the party by inviting someone she had a lot in common with. Urbana was also blonde, though of the platinum kind, and they were both going to be nurses. Unlike the other Bleu Moon girls, who wanted to be doctors and physical therapists, Urbana had been pursuing the same bachelor of science degree and knew what it was like to be a servant of many in the form of a nurse. Also, both Urbana and Yerma, had ties with those working for law enforcement. Yerma's father, Thiede McCallum, had been part of that workforce his entire life. He eventually became a well respected detective. Urbana would eventually marry an enforcing officer going by the name of Augustin Goldstone. She just did not know it yet.

Bleu Moon's plan for the night of Gair's birthday was to head over to So-Li Brewhouse, drink some drinks, and then come back to Bleu Moon where they would meet the Dixie Girls along with Malaney and Patsy. Gair's boyfriend, Kanhaiya Chargeant, had come all the way from the Southwestern part of the nation to join them on their walk to So-Li Brewhouse and have a good time at the house as well. So-Li was located about three blocks south of Bleu Moon, on the Eastern side of the road. This would provide Bleu Moon the perfect opportunity to inebriate Kaizen and hopefully, put him in a vulnerable enough position to gain more insightful information about him. They wanted to know what made Kaizen tick. They wanted to know if he could be inebriated to the point where perhaps one of the girls, be it the Bleu Moon Girls or the Dixie Girls, would get lucky with him that night. They also had something else, quite special, planned for him that night in case everything went according to plan.

Once Bleu Moon arrived at So-Li Brewhouse, they were greeted by an attractively pleasant and familiar face belonging to Senica Sidwell. Senica led them outside to wait for their table to be ready. Though often reserved, Kaizen had always been a big witty flirt, and fun to be around because of his animated nature. What made Kaizen especially amusing, was how respectful he always seemed when flirting with everyone. His flirtiness gave those that didn't deserve his attention a false sense of worth, and a boost of self-esteem to those that were accustomed to this sort of behavior. Kaizen knew this, and had a fun time knowing his attendance at Gair's birth celebration (which he viewed as a good deed in the form of community service) would warm a lot of hearts and make even more people weak at the knees.

Patsy sat next to Kaizen during their wait time and sized him up to see if he would be boyfriend material. Kaizen, naturally, acted coy. He didn't completely dismiss her so as to completely destroy her hope. When Kanhaiya stood up from his seat to get closer to Gair and turned his back for a split second, Kaizen quickly licked his index finger and pointed at Kanhaiya whilst making a 'zzzzz' sound to compliment Kanhaiya's lean anatomy as it looked like he worked so very hard for it. Gair hated this, but she kept it to herself. She hated that Kaizen wasn't in the least threatened by someone like Kanhaiya. Gair thought that she had been very clear when she made a move on Kaizen that summer, and hopefully one day, he would give her an excuse to break up with her boyfriend. "Kanhaiya is the only person I kiss" she had told Kaizen during the summer, right after she had let herself into his room and locked the door. This out of the blue comment had come after a series of compliments aimed at Kaizen's advertising agency, even once calling it his "well-conceived baby". Gair thought that maybe if she drew enough attention to her one piece cougar colored leotard during that one night in the summer... maybe if she convinced Kaizen that "everyone needs some companionship here and there"... maybe if she cornered Kaizen enough, leaving very little space between him and her while he was in bed... then maybe he could convince him to put a baby inside of her. Although she had not worn it for months, she told anyone and everyone she had an intrauterine device, especially guys she wanted to bed. Kaizen, being a man with a moral code, never conceded to such advances, especially with a girl like Gair.

The fact Kaizen was very indifferent towards Gair and Kanhaiya's relationship was very heartbreaking for Gair. She thought that maybe Kaizen would display an ounce of jealousy. She was also very disappointed at how painfully socially unaware Kanhaiya was all the time. Kanhaiya was, in some way, the opposite of Kaizen. Kanhaiya had lied about his height to keep playing collegiate football. At least Kaizen had a moral code. Still, Kaizen respected Kanhaiya's work ethic. It takes a lot to come all the way up north to visit a deceptive girlfriend. Though Kaizen felt bad for Kanhaiya, he didn't let this dampen the mood.

Once Senica was making her way over to notify Bleu Moon that their table was ready, Kaizen made a point of letting everyone know he was starstruck. She had been at Kaizen's birthday party, thanks to Fagan. So Kaizen called Fagan's attention and mouthed the words "Oh My God" while pretending to hide his face behind his own hand and playfully acting coy towards Senica. All Fagan could muster up was a weak chuckle. If Senica had really tried, she could have probably kept Kaizen's attention for more than a night. It was unfortunate, for her, that she had to wait tables that night. Otherwise, she would have tried to see what Kaizen was all about. At least that is what she told herself.

Once everyone was seated at their table, Kaizen continued to be an enhanced version of himself. So as to liven the mood, he made sure to flirt with everyone, or at least make an alluring face to everyone. Kaizen was forced to sit next to Lyon, which he didn't like. Lyon was a boy no one could ever take seriously, even for someone like Kaizen who respected all walks of life. Kaizen viewed Lyon as a coward. Everyone instinctively knew Lyon played for the other team, but he tried so hard to hide it. It was like if someone as straight as Kaizen pretended to not be straight, it would be odd and unbecoming. Lyon hated Kaizen, for he had the courage to be as honest as possible in all realms of life, whereas Lyon often hid his odd desires. This was another reason as to why not only Kaizen, but many other people, had no respect for someone like Chap who hid his heterosexuality.

So when Kaizen mockingly made kissy faces towards Lyon, Lyon reacted like any other coward would... he made his best attempt at seeming like a masculine guy by punching Kaizen's liver. Thankfully Kaizen was the best reflexes known to man, so in spite of being forced to be slightly inebriated, he rolled with the punch. Still in a righteously mocking manner, Kaizen playfully uttered "I could've died right there". Ruth Leslie, who was sitting in front of them, couldn't help but giggle. She couldn't wait to go back to the house to ruthlessly make herself known to Kaizen, no matter what it took. Malaney sat next to Ruth Leslie awkwardly. It was as if she wasn't even there.

Not long after Bleu Moon had arrived at So-Li and eaten their dinner, they decided to make their way back to the house. A party needed tending. Their quest back was sidetracked by a photobooth that attempted to suck everyone in.

The only immune one to these kinds of sentimental formalities was Kaizen. When everyone told him to get in at the last second, he pulled out a kissy face that made its way slowly to Yerma. Yerma could not hide her blushing face. She was, however, able to hide her intrusive thoughts... *Oh please, Kaizen, just do it already. What are you waiting for?! Put your lips on my cheek and make me yours!*

Beep... beep... cluck-cluck-cluck the photobooth quickly snapped. Kaizen stood up and said "Guess it's time to go!", leaving Yerma alone in her thoughts. She finally stood up, after being pushed out by everyone, and proceeded to follow them back to Bleu Moon.

As soon as Bleu Moon arrived back at headquarters, it didn't take long for the celebration to commence. The Dixie Girls were the first to start transporting themselves into the living room, attempting to find parking space for their well-fitted 'dumptrucks'. Given that Lyon & Chap had already cleared out the living room by moving all furniture to the sides, this was not a hard task for the Dixie Girls to accomplish. Fagan had excused himself to his bedroom as soon as the first invitees arrived. Patsy, Malaney and Urbana had already been at the house way before Bleu Moon arrived. They had been hovering in the kitchen, making it seem as if they were on some sort of patrol duty.

Chap ensured the LED RGBW strip lights were on and pulsating to provide ambience while he played his playlist. Chap had worked very hard on the playlist, a multiple week effort that did not disappoint. This provided the perfect environment for a small party. The Dixie Girls and Bleu Moon spent that night playing a few card games but mostly spent it with a bunch of dance games since the loud music defeated the purpose of a card game.

All of the dance games played that night, including Cha Cha Slide, was the perfect way to get everyone involved. This was because everyone there, in some way or another, was a dancer. Sage & Elsie were among the most attractive flyers in the school's cheerleading squad. Elsie was also part of the school's dance team, along with Lyon. The rest of the Dixie Girls enjoyed dancing as well, especially when Elsie taught them a few dance moves. Pretty much the entirety of Bleu Moon met each other during their first year dance class elective. Ruth Leslie remembered very clearly how smooth Kaizen could be on the dance floor. She reminisced about the time her first year dance class cohort had been invited to observe the other dance class cohort during finals week, of which Gair, Lyon, Kaizen and Urbana had been a part of. The most memorable dance presentation had been Kaizen and Urbana's group, mostly because of how out of their heads they were the entire time as well as the manner in which they had finished off the dance. Kaizen had kneeled, providing a sort of seat for Urbana to sit on and provide the audience with a 'grace face' pose. Every girl in that dance room had wanted to be Urbana at that moment. Kaizen didn't mind having Urbana sit on him, given that during her first year, she had been donning one of the most inviting bums in the school.

This memory, which had slivered into Ruth Leslie's head, seemed to have sparked something that made her feel extra girly that night during Gair's birthday. She could not stop thinking about Kaizen. She hoped that he had noticed her in her revealing outfit... nothing but a bra to cover her upper body, a blue bandana styled nicely around her head, and some light blue jeans to match her sneakers. She had changed as soon as she arrived back from So-Li Brewhouse. It was hard not to notice, not only for Kaizen, but for everyone else as well.

The most peculiar part during Gair's birthday that night had revealed itself during one of the dance games. It had come from a dance trend on ClickClock. Though it involved less touching than an Appalachian big circle dance routine, it somehow managed to be more obscene. The name of the trend is hard to remember. The beat, not so much. It included an inciting beat, a not so complicated yet still a crisis inducing three quick beats, followed by a climactic and resolutory beat. Something like *bwaaah bweeh-bweeh-bweeh boom... bwaaah bweeh-bweeh-bweeh boom... bwaaah bweeh-bweeh-bweeh boom...*

This ClickClock dance trend involved coming up with a dance move, and then doing another dance move that indicated you've passed the beat to someone else. Kind of like a 'pass the beat' dance. It was very childish. Though Kaizen was very good at it, he detested it. The one that liked this game very much but did not perform very well, was Lyon. When Lyon's turn had come, he pushed those closest to him in the circle to the side so there could be space for him to get on all fours and proceed to thrust his pelvis on the ground. Lyon thought everyone around the circle would find his 'humping-ground' abilities appealing. All this did was make everyone very uncomfortable.

Notably, though not by doing much, Kaizen drew the most attention during Gair's birthday that night. This was normal for Kaizen. Plus, there was a higher ratio of girls to guys, so he didn't take the situation very seriously given the unfairness of the situation. This, however, didn't stop Blaire Darton from screaming "Yesss Kai" every time she found the chance to do so. Eventually, she could not help herself but to go over to Kaizen, grab Kaizen by the hand and spin herself as if she were his girlfriend.

Who the fuck do you think you are Kaizen thought to himself while he very cordially spun her one last time and retreated from the dance game so he could make his way over to the kitchen for a breather. Once Kaizen crossed the beaded curtain decoration hanging from the head jamb of the kitchen, he noticed Ruth Leslie had followed him. She gave Kaizen a quick and subtly flirty smile before bending over to grab one of the red balloons that had stumbled onto the kitchen from the living room, making sure to take her sweet time on her way up, so as to give Kaizen a nice view of what could be his for the night. Everyone, even Kaizen, pretended not to notice this. In an attempt to shift the attention of the room during the current situation, Kaizen turned over to Urbana and asked "Were you able to see exactly how Fabienne tripped and fell?" Kaizen, was genuinely curious as he had been one of the few that did not get a glimpse of how Fabienne had tripped soon after arriving at Bleu Moon.

Although Urbana had seen it, she did not want to bring attention to it, so she began to shake her head. Milliseconds after Kaizen had verbally inquired and Urbana had physically responded, there was a high pitched *woop-woop* outside of the house. The boys in blue had arrived.

The Dixie Girls & Bleu Moon had come in contact with each other frequently due to shared clubs and activities, so coming in contact with each other at this indoor social gathering would not break any of the school's indoor social gathering restrictions. Plus, at 7 residents, Bleu Moon residents would technically already have been breaking these restrictions even though they had signed their lease agreement before the kungflu virus had caused all of the nation's restrictions and social panic.

Explaining all of these circumstances to a law enforcer, was something that no one wanted to do. At this moment, Bleu Moon, the Dixie Girls and other birthday party attendees had been presented with two bad choices... these choices were either confronting law enforcement amidst the widespread kungflu virus or avoiding law enforcement by either fleeing or hiding from the scene.

The LED RGBW strip lights went from a rapidly pulsating rainbow glow to a still white light. The torchiere light turned on and followed suit, revealing the creamy white inner walls of Bleu Moon. Patsy Chi was the first girl to run out of the kitchen side door. It seemed she had already developed an instinct for avoiding situations in which she could be blamed and become a victim. This stemmed from previously having lived with the Bleu Moon girls, who had found it quite easily to use her as a scapegoat during the most trying of times. Kanhaiya Chargeant left the kitchen and made his way upstairs to Gair's room. Fabienne Freckle had already left earlier that evening since she couldn't handle the embarrassment of being the only one of the Dixie Girls that could not pleasantly coordinate her hips in a dancing motion. Sage Burland, Taylor Hues, Britney Hues, Elsie Appleman, Cathy Blake, Havana Crosse and Blaire Darton followed the same path that Patsy had taken to leave the house. They too, had run faster than a speeding bullet. Malaney Carlson froze in the kitchen. Urbana had taken this opportunity to head downstairs to Fagan's room, and drain him of an even smaller masculine energy than the one Chap possessed. Lyon, Chap, Gair, Yerma, Ruth Leslie and Kaizen were the only ones to head towards the front door and confront the law enforcers.

Luckily, for Bleu Moon, the house technically belonged to the school. This meant that any disputes had to involve members of the school's campus security as well, which were standing about six feet southeast of the law enforcers. Yerma stood 'bravely' in front of Bleu Moon while Kaizen 'sandwiched' them by standing in the back and watching their six. The law enforcers requested Bleu Moon's student id cards, to which they complied. After receiving all of their cards, the law enforcers asked a lot of odd leading questions in hopes of knowing a little more about the members residing in the house.

One of the first questions asked included "Is it just the six of you at this indoor social gathering?", to which Gair unhesitantly responded "Yes". Expecting this answer, the law enforcer asked "So all of the other girls that just ran from your side door were not part of your little congregation, right? I'm going to need a little more information from you." The law enforcer asked a series of questions to each of the six Bleu Moon members standing outside that night, each one received one question regarding their student id. Almost all of the questions made sense. The only one that didn't was the one that was queried to Kaizen... "What's your middle name?". Given that this was a stupid question, and that Kaizen was positioned farthest away from the law enforcer, Kaizen took this opportunity to amuse himself and ask a perfectly valid question... "Could you repeat that again?".

"What is your middle name?" the law enforcer repeated himself. Who knew what was running through Ruth Leslie's mind at this moment when she decided to butt in and request if the officer could "please say it louder for the people in the back?" while backing up her buttocks and letting it sag on Kaizen's crotch. This made Kaizen very uncomfortable. The law enforcer irritatedly repeated himself for the last time... "What. Is. Your. Middle. Name?"

"Oh... I don't have one" Kaizen finally replied. The law enforcer gave the student id cards back once they had been recorded by the campus security. Soon after law enforcement and security left, Bleu Moon went back inside to flee from the prying eyes hidden behind the windows of their neighbors. They had a quick conversation attempting to figure out who had called the police.

Chap had exempted himself from any responsibility by stating "Okay guys, I know I called the po-po on Lyon and Fagan that other time, but I did not do that this time!" Everybody else released themselves from responsibility as well, however, in a more believable manner. After no one seemed to pinpoint a perpetrator, they called it a night and went to their rooms. Urbana had said bye to everyone as she headed out of the front door, but not before cleaning the white gunk dripping from the side of her lips with her sweater.

Gair's birthday was revelatory. It would prove to be more revelatory, once it was made known who had called law enforcement and why. The answers to those questions would show the true character of Bleu Moon.

Lyon scrolled through ClickClock that night before going to sleep. The length of the videos he watched that night averaged a length of about forty-five seconds. Lyone Measle's entry for the night within his cardboard covered wide-ruled composition notebook read...

09-18-2020

Today, the department of human services & health announced a plan to make all kungflu vaccines free for the nation!

Who makes the most money in broadcasting?!
WHAT does Kaizen Domina possess?!
Where is the safest place in a house to hide?!
When is the ideal time to request sex from a stranger?!
Why is the kungflu virus extremely deadly?!
How does one become a successful journalist?!
Which witch witched & whose whom?!

The Reliable Journalist?

Any time a house gathering or party of sorts gets
interrupted by the boys in blue, it is safe to assume
that they did not end up there by randomly
patrolling the streets. Unless of course, someone
within that social gathering circle is closely
connected to the law enforcing authorities, in
which case, it would be a solid bet to assume those
closest to the law enforcing authorities had
directly been the reason for the party to end
abruptly. Though Yerma, Urbana and even
Malaney (she slept around with the easiest
pickings the world has to offer, hence, explaining
her odd connections with law enforcement) had
deep connections with law enforcement, it was
not them who had called the boys in blue to crash
the party that night.

      On the Second October evening of the
year Two Thousand & Twenty, a couple of weeks
after Bleu Moon had hosted Gair Mallard's
birthday party... Lyon Measle was still unaware as
to why Radisson Quebec (Bleu Moon's neighbor)
had called the authorities to inform them there
was an indoor social gathering occurring that had
broken the school's indoor social gathering
restrictions. Lyon was even more unaware as to

why Yerma, Gair, Ruth Leslie and Chap had asked Radisson to call the authorities on them during the night of Gair's birthday.

At times of confusion, Lyon liked to go to Hack & Scam's Bar & Grill and ponder so deeply to the point where he got lost in his thoughts. Lyon felt that a few alcoholic drinks helped him do so. Although Hack & Scam's did not provide the best environment for any individual to come and think deep thoughts, Lyon thought it did. There was a sweet spot he liked getting to while drinking... the point where he didn't feel inhibited by anything and the point right before his motor cortex was completely affected. After all, Bleu Moon was a couple of blocks south and one block east from Hack & Scam's, making this habit feasible. At least feasible within the mind of Lyon Measle. Tonight, given that it had been awhile since he had been to Hack & Scam's, he spent a good portion of his time pondering about Bleu Moon related events occuring within the past couple of months. Despite the insurmountable evidence to the contrary, Lyon liked thinking of himself as a reliable narrator.

How could it be that someone like Kaizen Domina seems to be deemed so just and righteous in the eyes of those in commanding positions? Do the girls not care that he's fucked at least four girls whom he doesn't even spend so much time in public with? He doesn't even seem to care that other people know he's been with a multitude of girls. What a free man he must feel like. Imagine how many more other girls have been with him? This cannot be an innocent man. Quite clearly, he had something to do with law enforcement showing up that night on Gair's birthday. It was also very odd that all of the attention seemed to be on him, even though it was supposedly Gair's birthday party. I twerked for them, why didn't they give me any attention? Why didn't Kaizen give me any attention? I wish he was part of the members of my high school basketball team that sodomized me. Maybe I can turn him! But how can I do that?! He seems to be straight, given that he pulls a lot of attractive women. But how does he do it so effortlessly, other guys try so very hard and go so out of their way to even get with as many girls as Kaizen does. Maybe, if I bring him some girls, I could perhaps slip into the action myself! After all, the public thinks me and Carey have broken up, nobody, except some girls of course, suspect that Carey is basically my beard. Not even my own father knows I play for the other team! What a sucker. He doesn't even seem to care that I have a girlfriend with the same name as my own mother. I could be Oedipus and he would not bat an eye. I guess that is what one can expect from a neutered animal. A man with more money than most... and he spends it on chopping his own balls off just so he can fuck with more peace of mind. How pathetic! I have to give it *to Kaizen, I wish HE was my father. At least he does the sensible thing and fucks girls in the ass. I just wish he delved into the male market too, just so I can have a chance at him! But noooo. He doesn't even delve into the female market. He lets the female market come to him. What a fucking snob. The girls seem to adore him so very much. Why is the world so unjust? Let's see if the boys in blue give him any slack for having another indoor social gathering. I'll bring the female market to him this time!*

Not long after his last scheming thought, he went to work. He headed over to some girls who often patronized the Hack & Scam's establishment, which happened to be within the same graduating class as him, and let his glibness shine. Lyon was a wannabe in all realms of his life. This included journalism. Lyon was a wannabe journalist, through and through. This wannabe journalist managed to lure quite a few girls over to Bleu Moon. These girls were Miranda Ingrit, Patsy Chi, Cait Swab, Taylor Hues, Cait Flanigan and Dory Donlon among others. They knew Kaizen lived in the same house, otherwise, they wouldn't have given Lyon's proposal a second thought.

Their arrival at Bleu Moon wasn't subtle. Sure, Lyon wanted to give Kaizen some irresistible temptation to think about. But what Lyon felt like really doing, was to show everyone around the block who the 'Big Boss' or 'Head

Honcho' really was. He wanted to show them that no one could stop Bleu Moon from throwing as many parties as they desired. Especially 'spontaneous' ones like the one he had orchestrated tonight.

Soon after arriving at Bleu Moon, Lyon turned on the speaker and turned on the LED RGBW strip lights to the same rapidly pulsating rainbow glow setting they were on when law enforcement had showed up on the night of Gair Mallard's birthday party. Miranda, Taylor, Patsy and Cait Swab stood in the kitchen. Cait Flanigan and Dory Donlon stood in front of Kaizen and Fagan's bedrooms in the basement. The square patch of basement floor on which Cait Flanigan and Dory Donlon stood allowed for easy access to six different case openings, four of which had some sort of door. The two other case openings were located towards the East and Southeast from where they were standing. The Eastern case opening served as the upstairs while the other one served as a mini storage room. Within the storage room, there was a tankless water heater among the many miscellaneous objects. Fagan's room was located on the Western side while Kaizen's room was located in the Southwest. The bathroom was located on the Northeast, and next to it on what would be considered the North, there was an almost well hidden door with a paint job that matched the creamy white wall. If it wasn't for the door handle, one would not be able to see it was there nor that it led to the main service panel and other electrical components. Cait Flanigan and Dory Donlon didn't know this, but if they had cracked this hidden door open, they would be able to see an almost pitch black empty room.

Kaizen had heard lovely and familiar voices outside of his room, along with the annoying and often soliloquizing voice of Fagan. So Kaizen decided to cautiously engage. He stepped out of his room, discreetly locking it from inside before showing face, and greeted the girls with a soft yet charismatically potent smile as he closed his door.

"Oh wow, you live here?!" exclaimed Dory Donlon while initiating a quick bear hug with Kaizen where she placed her hands around his neck and smooshed her breasts on his navel area, giving Kaizen the only option of wrapping his hands around her waist. Girls like Dory were clever. She and Cait Flanigan were very close friends, though Cait Flanigan was taller and had a more athletic build which Kaizen found very appealing.

"Heyyy Kaizen" Cait Flanigan seductively whispered with her sultry voice while she gave Kaizen a side hug that projected a warm heartedly sly hand holding onto Kaizen's torso for longer than a typical friendly hug would have. Kaizen always loved it when a girl initiated her giving nature before doing any taking, so naturally, he repaid the favor by letting his hand naturally slip downwards to his side which gently slapped Cait Flanigan's 'A' shaped bum. Cait quickly and flirtatiously side eyed Kaizen.

Cait Flanigan had been in Kaizen's fall semester statistics class during their second year at Gorgonzola College. Cait sat at the second to last row in the back, near the middle aisle, by herself... until Kaizen had walked into the room and sat next to her. Though Kaizen was all business during all of his classes, he always greeted with either a warm "Hi" or a head nod to acknowledge her presence. Kaizen didn't do this with everyone, however, and Cait Flanigan noticed. Though it was very clear, at least to Kaizen, that he found Cait Flanigan's face and curvaceous body very swimmingly, he managed to control his innermost desires to ravage her (consensually, of course) right then and there on the table in front of everyone. It just wasn't very practical, nor prudent. Cait Flanigan could feel his masculine vibrations during the entirety of every class, and she admired Kaizen's self restraint. She even admired how he was able to withhold that same level of self restraint when her and Dory decided to sit next to him during their spring semester management and information systems class of their second year. Tonight, however, she wanted him to unleash his innermost masculine abilities, but just didn't know how to get him to do so. This crippling analysis always left girls like Cait Flanigan with no guys to keep them company, since girls like her came off as a little shy or uninteresting.

Kaizen moved onwards and upwards, to the main floor of Bleu Moon, where he passed by Miranda, Cait Swab and Patsy among other girls. Miranda Ingrit had been Kaizen's high school junior prom date and just like she did in high school, she ogled him as he passed by. Patsy, at this moment, had noticed how Kaizen seemed to attract every single girl that laid eyes on him. This somehow made her even more attracted to him. Right before stepping into the living room, Kaizen acknowledged Taylor Hues by gently grasping the inside of her inner arm while giving her a quick "hey". This reminded Taylor of the time he had stopped her during their first year at Gorgonzola, only to comment on how she had a "very intriguing look about her". This simple comment had made her panties wet for several weeks. Tonight, after Kaizen's quick acknowledgement, she knew she would have lots of sleepless nights for the weeks to come once more. She loved having that pleasantly startling feeling that Kaizen always aroused in her. She wished he didn't move so suddenly into the living room. He always seemed to be a man on a mission.

After entering the living room where

Lyon and Chap were stationed, he spotted Carey
Fong. Apparently, Carey had "broken up" with
Lyon very recently. She was not invited to this
spontaneous indoor gathering, but she was
congregating at a house nearby when she spotted
Lyon going into Bleu Moon with a crowd. She
figured it would be okay for her to stop by. She
thought everyone at Bleu Moon was aware that
Lyon and her were never an actual item, but
rather, used each other for positive outcomes from
their public relationship. Kaizen, due to his
disinterest, was unaware of this. However, unlike
Lyon who always pretended to be kind and
friendly, Kaizen had always been courteous to
anyone and everyone that was invited into Bleu
Moon. Naturally, he went over to Carey, like he
always did, and proceeded to repay her the same
friendly hug she always gave him. On his way
over, he stumbled on a lighting cord that
projected him forward into Carey's arms. He used
her to regain balance and apologized, saying
"Sorry, I tripped over that cord right there"
while pointing to the ground.

From Lyon and Chap's angle, this is not
what it looked like. To them, it looked like Kaizen
and Carey had full heartedly embraced
themselves, looked at each other very lovingly,
and then both smiled towards the direction of
where Kaizen was pointing. From Lyon and
Chap's angle, it looked like they were reminiscing

about a time they had partaken in some 'headboarding' action in Kaizen's bedroom. Chap took this opportunity to use Lyon's superiority complex against Kaizen by enthusiastically whispering to Lyon, "He totally ROMPED your girl's RUMP to smithereens... in your basement!"

Lyon's face went from smug undertones, to blank, to a red hue that fully revealed his rage for being deemed as a joke when being compared to Kaizen. Perhaps it was an overcompensation for Lyon's secret degradation fantasies. Perhaps he just hated being embarrassed in public. Perhaps it was because his plans to selfishly couple Kaizen with some party girl that was not Carey had gone awry. If Carey and Kaizen had been bumping uglies, it would not be good publicity for Lyon. Before storming into his room like a little kid, his thoughts followed suit...

First Caroline Wilkinson. Then, Yerma Mayda. Then, Faye The Firefighter. Then, Boni Alderson. God knows who else! And now Carey, "My Carey"... too?! This guy needs to save some for the rest of the men lining up for dessert. What does Kaizen Domina have that I don't?!!! Life can be so unfair! He doesn't even workout!

The last eventful incident of this short night was when Kaizen made his way back to his room. As he passed the kitchen, he noticed Cait Swab was standing outside on the porch. Kaizen approached to inquire... "why have you been stalking me?" This startled Cait Swab quite a bit as she didn't know how to answer that. They both found each other extremely attractive. Kaizen wouldn't mind bending her over a barrel at that moment and showing her the many states of the nation. In fact, he would love it and she had always had a feeling this was true. The problem was whether or not Cait Swab would stop beating around the bush or do something about her affection towards Kaizen. Tonight, she decided to grab Kaizen from the shoulder while playfully pinning him against the wall only to tell him... "We need to talk later".

Later never came. Cait Swab failed to seize her opportunity with Kaizen. She would long for him for years to come. She felt, deep inside her heart, that Kaizen was "The One". Then again, so did many other girls. She was not unique when it came to such a sentiment.

While Kaizen was metaphorically breaking necks with his suave maneuvers back into his room located in the basement, Lyon was upstairs in his room already scrolling through ClickClock once more. The length of the videos he watched that night averaged a length of about forty seconds. Lyon Measle's entry for the night within his cardboard covered wide-ruled composition notebook read...

10-02-2020

Today, the nation's president tested positive for
the kungflu virus!

Who makes the most money, broadcasters or
marketers?!
What DOES Kaizen Domina possess?!
Where do most people hide their banking details?!
When will life throw me a bone?!
Why is life so unfair to me?!
How can I be better?!
Which witch witched & whose whom?!

Circle of 'Angels'

On the Sixth October evening of the year Two
Thousand & Twenty... Bleu Moon residents
congregate in the common area of the house,
where everyone can see each other in the face.
Lyon was erroneously convinced and outraged at
Kaizen for calling the cops on them that night.
Lyon was even more outraged at Kaizen for
ruining his reputation by bonking Carey Fong in
the basement. Or so he thought. Kaizen would not
let someone like Carey into his 'no-no square'.
This outrage distracted Lyon from the purpose of
Bleu Moon's congregation that evening... to
figure out how to go into the school hearing for
the 'widespread virus restrictions violated' during
Gair Mallard's birthday party.

     This hearing complicated Bleu Moon's
reputation, not only in the eyes of Gorgonzola,
but in the eyes of their peers as well. If the
restrictions had been well thought out, they
would have accounted for houses like Bleu Moon,
which would be in violation by default given the
seven people that were inhabiting the premises
already. Another thing that had not helped out,
was the decision of the representatives of
Gorgonzola to interview the individuals of Bleu

Moon in separate groups about the events that had occurred that night, creating a sort of prisoner's dilemma among them. Thankfully they had a bit of time to decide how they would present the events occurred during the evening of Gair Mallard's birthday celebration.

However, a portion of the birthday party attendees had indiscreetly fled the party scene when law enforcement showed up during the party. No restrictions would have been violated since many of Bleu Moon's members interacted with them daily via many shared activities, it just would not look very good when trying to explain it to the eyes of the authorities. Bleu Moon could either say it was already impractical to follow widespread virus restrictions or that only a few additional attendees had been present at the birthday party that evening... both options not being the best of choices.

At this moment, Gair, Yerma, Ruth Leslie and Chap wished they wouldn't have told Radisson Quebec to call the cops on them that night. They wanted to see if Kaizen would express any sort of allegiance to the house, even in moments of crisis. They mostly wanted to find out which one of the birthday party attendees tickled his fancy. It would have been amusing for them to see Kaizen fall into temptation only to have his intimate moments be crashed by the lowly authorities. Unfortunately for them, they had never come across a man with this much integrity in their entire life. They should have known Kaizen would not fall for unbecoming vulgarities which could be excused, at least in their minds, through the guise of inebriation.

The Bleu Moon girls wished that Lyon had not summoned more people into the house. An act that would most likely not have been triggered if they would just have told Lyon and Fagan what would happen that night beforehand, and why they were doing it in the first place. Truth was, they all wanted to shag Kaizen, but were just too afraid to let Lyon or Fagan know because Lyon always made it seem like he was good buddies with Kaizen and Fagan, so by letting them know they were really into Kaizen the Bleu Moon girls would risk having their feelings divulged to Kaizen. It was true that Lyon had a good relationship with Fagan, given that Fagan liked being glorified in a puppy like manner which Lyon was so well adept in doing. Kaizen, however, felt indifferent towards Lyon. If the Bleu Moon girls had known this, it would have put their conundrum to rest.

Perhaps all of this holy premeditation had no purpose. Perhaps this congregation was all for nothing. Perhaps they had met with each other in vain and wasting time that they could be doing homework or getting involved in endeavors that would shape their careers. And although this would be the case, as the school representatives would just end up telling them "they were adults and could make their own decisions by themselves"... Bleu Moon just didn't know this would be the way the cards would pan out.

Gair suggested they all declare there had only been a few additional attendees present at the birthday party. Ruth Leslie, Yerma and Chap expressed their approval with this suggestion out loud. Kaizen suggested that no specifics be divulged and to declare that no sound restrictions were violated, which would have been the righteous way to go into the meetings with the school representatives. Lyon and Fagan internally agreed, but decided to show an external agreement with Gair. Kaizen reluctantly agreed with everyone, claiming that he'll let the others do most of the talking during the meeting. After this decision was agreed upon, all but Lyon, Chap and Gair left the common room.

"Look, Lyon, don't get mad at us, but really, it was us who told Radisson to call the cops that night on my birthday. We just wanted to see if our friends were really our friends, you know." Gair told Lyon, while Chap stood as witness.

"I understand. We still go into the meeting as planned, correct? Kaizen will be there during my meeting, which means I'll be doing most of the talking."

"Oh yes, that's the plan!" Chap declared.

"By the way, whose credit card is this?" Lyon asked as he picked up a shiny card laying on the floor.

"It looks like it belongs to Kaizen's company", Lyon answered his own question as he put it on the coffee table.

"We should all probably head back to our rooms and get some good rest, we have a big day ahead of us tomorrow. You should probably leave that there, Kaizen will probably come looking for it pretty soon..." Gair chirped in a scoldingly manner as she headed up the stairs and into her room.

Chap followed suit and went into his own room. Lyon stayed in the common room for a bit, pretending to watch a bit of tv. While everyone was back in their rooms... Lyon stayed in the living room for a sitcom episode's length... enough time for him to take a picture of the front and back of Kaizen's credit card. His inner thoughts found this to be a blessing.

I will show Kaizen that he is not above any moral law. It doesn't matter that it wasn't him that called the authorities, he will pay for making me look like a chump. No one fucks my pretend girlfriend and doesn't suffer any consequences for doing so. Everyone will know what happens once you mess with Lyon's pretend girlfriend. Once Kaizen comes out complaining about his credit card charges, no one will ever try to mess with me again! Lyon used

Kaizen's credit card information in what he considered a very lavish manner soon after this evening. After all, he also had memorized Kaizen's four digit pin from a time when they had been out and about together earlier that year.

Kaizen would eventually notice this financial discrepancy when making entries into his ledger account after finding his financial card the next morning. To Kaizen, it would be obvious who the idiot that tried to wrong him was, but he decided not to do anything about it just yet... given the laughable, yet significant amount to many, by which this individual tried to wrong him with. After his criminal spending spree, Lyon took out his phone and his cardboard covered wide-ruled composition notebook. The length of ClickClock videos he watched that night averaged a length of about thirty-five seconds. This night, his notebook entry read...

10-06-2020

Food insecurity in the nation reached 52 million due to the kungflu virus!

Who is most likely to suffer during a food shortage?!
What does KAIZEN Domina possess?!
Where is the best place to hide other people's banking details?!
When does the stomach begin to eat itself?!

Why can humans not exist without food?!
How much food is too much?!
Which witch witched & whose whom?!

On the Seventh October morning of the year Two
Thousand & Twenty... the ambiance within Bleu
Moon felt a little less playful... a little less
perky.... a little less nonchalant. Among the Bleu
Moon girls and Bleu Moon boys... there was a
greater sense of solidarity after going into the
school hearing with representatives from
Gorgonzola. Another attribute that could be
sensed within the group of Bleu Moon boys and
the Bleu Moon girls was fear... for the kungflu
virus. The fact they had to go into a meeting,
made these boys and girls take the virus with an
exponentially greater sense of seriousness than
they had before. Kaizen, on the other hand,
seemed to be his same self. He walked the same
walk. Ate the same food. And even pooped the
same poop as he always did. The habits of both
the Bleu Moon boys and girls however, seemed to
fluctuate even more after this meeting with the
school's representatives.

One could hardly blame these boys and
girls. After all, more and more cases of the
widespread virus had been manifesting through
their friends, families and close ones. The thing
that these boys and girls secretly admired about
Kaizen, the man, was this carelessness he seemed

to walk through life with. It had been incredibly inspiring in various moments of their time together. But, there comes a point in time when certain outlooks on life's peculiar circumstances clash with each other, and perhaps further complicate the situation at hand. This was one of those moments. Kaizen's attitude and behavior seemed bizarre. Foolish, even. At least in the eyes of these boys and girls that could not fathom a world without constant human interaction. Kaizen was used to this environment. He thrived in it. Everyone else's life goals were not congruent with a life not filled with constant human interaction.

Most of Bleu Moon, barring Kaizen, wanted to go into a physical therapy field... where constant touching would be involved when dealing with a patient. Or the nursing field... where constant communication and good bedside manner would be required. Or journalism... where a deep connection with the material source is ideal. Or the communication field... a field that requires more than one singularity to exist. It was because of these passions and desires that they deemed Kaizen's behavior quite insane. Clearly, they had to go back into their sense of normalcy in order for their world to exist. If they went about their days as Kaizen did, they would not be contributing to get back their world as they would be doing 'nothing' to change the situation. These boys and girls could continue to do nothing, or submit to nationwide requirements that allowed for their world to be pieced back together. To these boys and girls, the choice was clear. They would do whatever it takes to get everyone in the house tested for the kungflu virus, no matter how tyrannical their efforts may be.

No one in Bleu Moon had taken the virus quite seriously, even when reinfections were confirmed in Kon Hon towards the end of August. When the department of human services & health announced a plan to make all kungflu vaccines free for the nation, they had paid it no mind. Mostly because they were too busy partaking in Gair Mallard's birthday party. When the nation's president tested positive for the kungflu virus at the beginning of October, they found it amusing. They felt it was comedy. Now, fifty two million people in the nation had reached a feeling of food insecurity and the school had just pressed Bleu Moon about the events of Gair Mallard's birthday to get a sense of how many restrictions were being broken. The Bleu Moon boys and girls would deem it brave to continue doing nothing amidst the rising cases of kungflu virus among their friends, family and close ones. Hence, they defaulted to the decision of tyrannically getting everyone in the house tested.

The Bleu Moon girls felt that given the fact they had already been able to get away with lying about their intentions behind Gair's finely orchestrated birthday celebration, they would be merited to continue to summon similar events and extravagances. Even though Lyon had not done so for the aforementioned reasons, his 'spontaneous' party orchestration after being questioned by law enforcement had actually made the Bleu Moon boys and girls look less guilty of any underhanded intentions among their unaware peers. So forcing everyone in the house to get tested for the kungflu virus would be nothing more than another event to them.

All this really meant, for their future, was a clash between their worldview and Kaizen's righteous ideals. It would raise a question of morality. A question of who is right and who is wrong, the collective of many or the few individuals like Kaizen. At first glance, either route would seem like it may not be hurting anyone. But the deeper one looks at the situation, the more clear it was that the collective of many had made it about which choice hurts less 'individuals'. In other words, the Bleu Moon boys and girls did not care about the principles behind their actions, but rather, cared more about getting the right flavor of candy from the lollipop jar.

When the idea of forcing Kaizen into the nearest kungflu virus testing clinic site came about between the Bleu Moon girls this morning, Ruth Leslie knew it was her calling. She wanted to get back at Kaizen for not returning her unsolicited advances that night at Gair Mallard's birthday. She recruited Patsy Chi to accompany her on her escorting efforts. She had texted Patsy, letting her know that she was going to get tested that night before listening to the results of the school's hearing. The key part of her message was that Kaizen might come with them. This excited Patsy just as much if not more than Ruth Leslie. No greater honor could be felt by people like Ruth Leslie than making somebody else submit against their will when matters of disagreement arose. It was her odd kink.

 Right after lunch, after everyone had partaken in the school hearing... Ruth Leslie sent Kaizen a text message inquiring about whether or not he would like to go and get tested for the novel kungflu virus. Kaizen, being the busy businessman he was, had taken a couple of hours to respond to her text with a plain and simple "sure". This caught Ruth Leslie a bit off guard, not because he had messaged her right before the time her and Patsy had agreed to head over to the testing site, but rather, because of the lack of struggle it took in getting him to agree to such an invitation. Both she and Patsy thought it might have been much harder to deviate a man like Kaizen from his path.

 Truth was, Kaizen could see how futile all of this testing was. He knew once an individual begins to get tested for a disease, real or not, this individual opens up himself for more opportunities to be diagnosed with diseases that may or may not exist. Otherwise, the field of psychology would not even exist. To him, it was basic marketing aims at influencing human behavior. He just wanted to get it over with, making sure this was the first and final medical test dispersed to him during his adulthood.

After coming back from taking the test, Ruth Leslie let her wickedly unchecked behavior be kindled by Kaizen's handsomeness. Before stepping into Bleu Moon that night, she purposefully stopped and bent over abruptly to pick up her phone, just so that Kaizen would bump into her with his giant crotch. It was hard to discern what was more unbecoming... her conviction to keep instigating an event that would never occur between her and Kaizen... or the fact that she dropped her phone after she abruptly stopped and bent over. Her unreasonableness, however, didn't stop there.

The morning after Bleu Moon had received the great 'no consequences' news from the school's representatives... Fagan Fogarty texted everyone that he had contracted the kungflu virus. This made everyone panicky. Given that Kaizen lived right next to Fagan, Ruth Leslie took the opportunity to ask, via text message, "what were the results for your kungflu virus test?". She had an insatiable desire to fornicate with Kaizen, but she didn't want to contract the kungflu virus and yield her career in the physical therapy field. Kaizen merely replied "you first" and put his phone away so he could continue to work on his business. Ruth Leslie didn't like being told what to do. She told everyone else that Kaizen had contracted the kungflu virus. This scared the rest of Bleu Moon, giving Yerma and Lyon the false right to head over to the basement with a disinfectant spray and threaten Kaizen to open the door so he could be disinfected and be quarantined at a different location that was not Bleu Moon. To their dismay, he opened the door and showed them his results, letting them know he had not contracted any virus. Unlike the rest of the Bleu Moon boys and girls, Kaizen had an indomitable will that prevented him from falling to such apocalyptic self-fulfilling prophecies. This was one of the reasons as to why Kaizen was the man of that house, and every house he lived in thereafter.

After unsuccessfully making Kaizen look like a fool with the help of Yerma, Lyon went into his room and proceeded to take out his phone and his cardboard covered wide-ruled composition notebook. The length of ClickClock videos he watched that night averaged a length of about thirty seconds. Tonight, his notebook entry read...

10-07-2020

New Sealand lifts restrictions and declares the
kungflu virus beaten on 10-7-20!

Who is immune to the kungflu virus?!
What does Kaizen DOMINA possess?!
Where did the kungflu virus originate?!
When will there be an end to this madness?!
Why do the rich get richer and the poor get
poorer?!
How does one become immune to the kungflu
virus?!
Which witch witched & whose whom?!

6 Feet Deep

On the Fourth November evening of the year
Two Thousand & Twenty... Lyon Measle's
unconscious self-awareness prevailed and was
chugging along, until Lyon himself began to
question what Kaizen really thought of him. More
specifically, he wanted to know what the weigh in
was when comparing their social, personal and
professional accolades. Lyon had always thought
of himself as a good looking wealthy casanova of
sorts... but the more time went on in the shadow of
someone like Kaizen, the more he started to
question himself as to what others thought of him.
No one could blame him. Kaizen always had this
effect on common people like Lyon. It was both a
gift and a curse. A gift in the sense that individuals
like Lyon finally understood what they actually
embodied as a person. A curse in the sense that
these revelatory thoughts often didn't bring about
much likability points for Kaizen. Thankfully, for
Kaizen at least, he had no political career
aspirations.

In the mind of Lyon, a false belief of
superiority never quite allowed him to interact
properly with Kaizen. Or anybody else for that
matter. Lyon was just not the most aware tool in

the shed. He had always pretended to be nice, in hopes of not burning any bridges Kaizen might someday provide with powerful and influential figures. But, Lyon's niceness always came at a cost for others. This cost came in the form of making the other individuals he addressed feel as if he was still 'above you' so to speak. There was always an air of 'I'm being nice, but you don't matter' that he carried with everyone. It was very off putting and awkward. Especially when he was nowhere near any high social ranks. Kaizen could never quite sense this snobbery when around him, mostly because he didn't pay much attention to individuals like Lyon. And if he had noticed these false pretenses, an acceptance of inferiority was not something he was going to allow.

Lyon felt that Kaizen, just by merely existing, had always complicated any favorable situation that came his way. Including Lyon's notion of high self-worth. Tonight, it was just the two of them inside of Bleu Moon. Lyon worries about Kaizen's perception of him, so he figures tonight might be a good opportunity to test the waters and see if Kaizen is worth addressing and keeping around. After all, if anything unfavorable occurs, thanksgiving break is just around the corner, providing time and space away from unpleasant situations should it be necessary. When Lyon was cooking his steak with asparagus that night, Kaizen came around the kitchen to head into the living room and watch a bit of tv.

Lyon never understood why people liked Kaizen so much. He was very reserved. Never really engaged much in conversation, and was very brief and short with any sort of social interaction. He was the antithesis of Lyon. Lyon often spoke without thinking, and frequented as many social gatherings he could get himself into. He didn't have any real-world aspirations, and he spent most of his time in the gym. Lyon was past the point of attempting to attain any sort of attention from Kaizen, but he was still infuriated at the notion of Kaizen hooking up with 'his Carey'. *How could he sit there watching tv in front of me as if nothing is happening*, Lyon thought. Given all of these circumstances, Lyon tried engaging in conversation with Kaizen while gnawing at his steak.

Lyon wanted to talk about something that would eventually lead into something that made him appear superior. Clearly, he was the most extroverted of the two, and as such, he felt that he might even be more traveled as well. So, he told him about future plans he had with some friends that involved going to a beach located at the state just below. For Lyon, the beauty of this state was that there were no taxes that had to be paid. Kaizen merely acknowledged how great of a plan it was and how it was a nice beach the last time he went there. Lyon couldn't stand how nonchalant he always was with his conversations. He wanted to push Kaizen's buttons, but didn't seem to know how.

Lyon's malicious intentions would eventually come back around to haunt him. Lyon would think about this conversation during his last moments alive. In those last moments, he would remember every other route he could have taken instead of wasting his time trying to move an immovable mountain like Kaizen. During Lyon's last moments, he would look back at this moment and realize that Kaizen was the individual he truly wanted to be. An unwavering beacon of hope. A symbol that no matter how hard life can be, there is indeed a way to overcome insurmountable odds. Lyon would remember the following remark during his last pleasure filled breath.

"You know, one day, I'll make my own company and I'll call it Médias Grandment Glorifiés". This was an attempted jab at Kaizen's very successful online digital advertising agency, going by the name of 'Media Glorifié'. Lyon thought that anyone could do what Kaizen did successfully. In Lyon's mind, all you had to do was perhaps make some cool videos with some cool words and post it via all social media channels. Lyon, was not a copywriter. He was barely a journalist, if that. Lyon was from a very different world than where Kaizen came from.

Kaizen was bred to bring his clients results. Lyon was bred to continue living like a child. In Lyon's mind, all you had to do to be successful was to have connections with influential people.

This was taught to him at a very early age from his parents. Lyon's father, Becker Measle, was a vice president of real estate transactions at a low tier land management company. Lyon's mother, Carey Measle, was a cake decorator. They thrived on getting to know highly intimate information about their clients, especially his mother. Lyon learned his cunning ways from his mother. He loved her so very much. So much so, he attained a fake girlfriend named after her. The best thing Lyon learned from his mother was to appear very innocent in the eyes of the public. This way, they would not suspect them of any wrongdoings. People like Kaizen, could see through Lyon's 'innocent' façade.

As such, Kaizen merely replied "do it" to Lyon's idiotic comment. Kaizen knew what Lyon didn't, which was that no matter who you are, what you do, when you were born, where you live and why one does what they do... no external influence will dictate your success better than the internal influence that lives inside the individual day after day. After all, external influences aren't always there and they only last so long. There is indeed an expiration date to precious resources. The best resource one can depend on is the one given by the higher being, if there is one. Which is oneself. It was as if all of this reasoning had finally crept up into the mind of Lyon. It was as if someone had just buried him six feet deep underground and carved his name on the stone atop his grave. That someone was Lyon himself.

Lyon decided that he would no longer pretend to be nice to Kaizen. It was clear, to everyone, that Kaizen was the superior individual. Lyon just couldn't wrap his mind around this. He went into his room, half choking on his steak and asparagus. He proceeded to pull out his phone and his cardboard covered wide-ruled composition notebook. The length of ClickClock videos he watched that night averaged a length of about twenty-five seconds. Tonight, his notebook entry read...

11-04-2020

The nation reports 100,000 new cases of the kungflu virus in 24 hours!

Who let the dogs out?!
What does Kaizen Domina POSSESS?!
Where do most cases of kungflu virus originate?!
When will I see the light at the end of the tunnel?!
Why am I not beautiful but just damned?!
How can I be more beautiful?!
Which witch witched & whose whom?!

Frenemiessss

On the Eleventh November evening of the year Two Thousand & Twenty... Lyon decided to postpone his decision on completely halting his pretense of being nice towards Kaizen. He just couldn't help himself, being a shammer was rooted deep within his nature, passed down from generation to generation. Besides, he wanted to hold off on this decision mostly because he wanted to extract some more information from Kaizen. Information that could be beneficial in making him look like a fool. He wanted to extract information that could ruin Kaizen's reputation with any future lady prospects.

There was a slight complication however, he just couldn't show up with the same level of politeness that he had shown up with before. He felt his last interaction with Kaizen was a little rocky, given that it did not go as he had planned. Lyon wanted to make Kaizen feel that he was below not only Lyon himself, but from others as well. Lyon felt Kaizen's disacknowledgement of Lyon's self-deemed superiority merited premeditated wrongs. So, Lyon ensured that Kaizen knew he had tried to invite everyone and their mom to a drive-in movie theater. He did so by complaining about everyone's unavailability to Bleu Moon's walls, pretending that he hoped someone from Bleu Moon would accompany him. However, everyone of the Bleu Moon boys and Bleu Moon girls pretended not to be available for a drive-in-theater spectacle hosted by a local broadcasting company. This allowed for the last minute invitation during dinner time extended to Kaizen to appear as something that was an afterthought. A perfect setup for Lyon's status quest. He couldn't wait to see Kaizen take the bait.

The drive-in movie theater was located at 19619 E. Giraldo Liberty Pond, Warrington 66079, which was more than fifteen minutes from Bleu Moon. When the invitation was extended, Kaizen was already more or less prepared with how to respond to such an invitation, as he had always been prepared to respond to other such invitations. First off, Kaizen was a fruitarian that prepared his meals at least a week ahead of time. His meal preparation was merely a process of buying specific ingredients that could be eaten straight out of the packaging. Specific types of herbs and spices contained in glass containers with certain kinds of nuts and canned beans comprised Kaizen's everyday magic formula. As ridiculous as it may sound, he was more fit than any professional athlete without ever having to work out. He didn't seem like it at first glance however. Kaizen used this excuse of already having his meals prepared so he wouldn't be bothered to get out of his weekly rhythm. This time however, although Kaizen had used this excuse at first, he eventually gave into the invitation. He believed it would be amusing to accept this invitation, in a rather unconventional way.

Although Lyon was a complete shammer, he was completely predictable to individuals like Kaizen. From the very first moment Kaizen had met Lyon, he had already sensed his false nature. You see, Lyon always began to form more animated gestures, both facial and physical whenever he was acting fraudulently. This was noticeable when Lyon yelled across the living room to address Kaizen right before The Hawt Seat game. This was also noticeable when Lyon had disgustingly twerked in the middle of the circle during Gair Mallard's birthday. It was also noticeable when Lyon had 'spontaneously' invited people from Hack & Scam's over to Bleu Moon for a quick social gathering. This fake façade has been extremely noticeable to Kaizen lately. So as to avoid risking the four digit pin that allowed cash withdrawals from his bank, Kaizen's grocery shopping days with Lyon or any other individual stopped from then on, since there was absolutely no doubt to Kaizen, or any other higher being, that Lyon had been the one using his banking card quite extravagantly.

So when Lyon extended an invitation for this movie viewing experience, Kaizen knew it would be amusing to see just how stupid Lyon thought Kaizen was. It would be very amusing to see how much Lyon thought Kaizen didn't know had already been planned with the rest of the house as to the types of information that was planned to be extracted from him by pretending to be Kaizen's dearest friend. It would be amusing for Kaizen to see just how idiotic everyone pretended not to be. What would be most amusing, was to see the idiots everyone knew as the Bleu Moon boys and girls get a sense of superiority when being cross-ranked with Kaizen. After all, Kaizen could afford to do so. They couldn't. The Bleu Moon boys and girls were brave amateurs. There is nothing more amusing than seeing a snake finally catch something, after going months without eating. These snakes are so hungry, they suffocate while they're eating.

To Lyon, his public image was everything. His joie de vivre was rooted in his public image. He had to make it known that everybody liked him while he, even though quite the opposite was the case, didn't think anything of anyone. Nobody really liked him. They tolerated him if they ever had the displeasure of meeting him. He spent so much time thinking about what other people thought about him that he convinced himself that everyone thought about him all the time. Truth was, no one really cared so much about him enough to think this long and hard about him. Those that did, were the unfortunate ones that had to deal with his nuisance day after day. Like Kaizen. This false sense of worth would contribute to that which would end up costing Lyon his life.

Tonight, Lyon's degradation fantasy got the best of him. He oddly liked it when someone made him feel like an unwanted pest. Perhaps, if psychology were true and correct, one could say it had something to do with the time he spent getting sodomized by his high school basketball team. So when Kaizen unknowingly triggered this emotion when he made it known that he was only going because no one else wanted to, Lyon almost lost sight as to why he was taking Kaizen to the drive-in movie theater in the first place.

Lyon had come to an agreement with the Bleu Moon girls. They had agreed to convince Fagan to sodomize Lyon in exchange for having Lyon be some sort of middle man for the girls. The girls still wanted to know where they stood in relation to Kaizen's sexuality. In other words, the Bleu Moon girls wanted to see if they were appealing enough to be sodomized by Kaizen. Funny the way things turn out. They wanted to know what Kaizen actually thought of them. They felt their best chance at getting this type of information was through Lyon. After all, Lyon had always made it seem like they were the best of buds.

This agreement seemed like a win-win-win for Lyon. He would get insight on Kaizen. He would be able to satisfy his fantasy by none other than the worst vermin the world has to offer... Fagan Fogarty. And he would seem like a superhero in the eyes of the Bleu Moon girls. There was no better feeling for Lyon than feeding three birds with one scone.

After gathering their keys, wallet, phone and quickly preparing themselves to watch a film about a group of kids who play baseball at a sandlot, they made their way into Lyon's white box on wheels. This car, if one could call it that, was named 'Sole' and manufactured by Hope Motor Company. It was a car that was on brand with Lyon Measle, given that he was like a piece of sticky gum that liked to be stomped by the sole of a shoe. Hopelessness drove Lyon to make this white box on wheels his vehicle. Now the only thing keeping Lyon's prying venture intact was Kaizen's ability to not laugh and keep his composure while riding what felt like a go-kart. Lyon tried to project his own shortcomings onto Kaizen by questioning him.

"How could you treat people as if they are below you and you are someone whose time is just too valuable? You're so uncultured", Lyon grunted.

"Well if the boot fits!", Kaizen remarked.

"See, like that... the expression is 'If the shoe fits'", Lyon pointed out.

"So you've never seen the 'Action Figure Allegory' film?!", Kaizen astoundedly questioned.

Kaizen totally caught Lyon off guard with said question, which led to both of them chuckling at this quick interaction. Here, Lyon was trying to smoothly transition into his prying venture by calling Kaizen uncultured in hopes of disarming him, yet here he also was, barely getting the reference to the first feature-length film to be made entirely using computer-generated imagery which starred astronaut and sheriff figurines. Lyon was just not as refined as Kaizen, but he ignored this. He continued to pry by changing the subject...

"So, what do you think of Rylie and Yerma?", Lyon asked, feeling like he had a good sense of how Kaizen would respond.

"What do you mean what do I think?", Kaizen replied.

"You know, which one would you...", Lyon began to question.

"Canoodle?", Kaizen Laughingly interrupted. "Well neither really, Rylie is kind of a disappointment. Her head is in the clouds if you ask me, and she does not have much going on. Yerma, although she does SEEM to take good care of herself, is just very insecure and her exercising habits reflect that, you know? Working out is a man made thing, and anyone willingly stepping into a room full of metal for the purpose of sweating for a very prolonged time is bound to be miserable. I just know she would not be a good time for me."

   This was not what Lyon expected out of Kaizen. Lyon totally thought Kaizen would at least show some sort of attraction towards Ruth Leslie, after all she was the easiest picking and most promiscuous one who was well known for making advances at anything and everything, so surely she had to have already made several tempting advances towards Kaizen. Though Kaizen found Ruth Leslie's demeanor to be cute, it wasn't something necessarily to be proud of, at least for Ruth Leslie. You see, a panda is cute. Would anyone do anything beyond hugging it platonically, if that? Most likely not. Everything that Kaizen had just told Lyon was perfect ammunition to use against him. Lyon could totally choose to keep all of this information to himself, and just tell the girls that Kaizen was into some very kinky stuff that they would probably not desire to partake in. But telling them exactly what Kaizen had said would surely be more than enough to make Kaizen's life a living hell. There was no bad choice here for Lyon, either way, the Bleu Moon girls would surely despise Kaizen after these remarks.

When Ruth Leslie was a young cub, during her adolescence, more specifically, her elementary school years... a peculiar nickname was given to her. She had told Patsy, Gair and even Yerma about this particular event. There was this boy, whom she found very attractive at the time, that always took up a prolonged duration of time in her daydreams. One day, she finally mustered up the courage to say hi to this young attractive boy, only to be greeted with a "Hi Rylie" by him. This was devastating for her, so she quickly corrected him by saying "My name is Ruth Leslie, not Rylie". The attractive young boy replied, "Listen Rylie, no one likes addressing a person if it takes more than a few syllables to do so. Plus, it suits you very well, given that it requires a lot of bravery and courage from a tiny person like you to walk around like they own the place. Which is exactly what you did when you hollered at me." Or something like that.

Point is, this nickname stuck. It actually did more than that. It spread. Everyone called her Rylie during her pre-undergrad school years, so that when she came to college and everyone had difficulty pronouncing her full name, she just told people to call her Rylie since it was easier to pronounce and it held a very special place in her heart. It reminded her of one of the very first guys that had managed to metaphorically shatter her heart, and in turn, have an antagonistic view of men. She was very emotional that way. It explains her endless pursuit of sexual validation, hence why she is willing to do anything and everything to every guy she can lay her hands on. Even if that guy is a little tiny feminine ball of energy stuck in the body of a giant. Like Chap.

Some of the Bleu Moon boys & girls still made the effort to call her by her full name, but Rylie just rolled off the tongue better. It was interchangeable really. You could tell just who really valued Ruth Leslie as a person by the way they addressed her. Those that either didn't pay her any mind, or were too interested in conserving their energy just merely addressed her in the easiest, most normal way possible. Whereas, those that often disperse an air that screams "I'm so politically correct and holier than thou", often defaulted to her full name. Sometimes, just to place the cherry on top, they even pronounced her last name. Ruth Leslie Lyon. Those three names, said in that order of primacy, just fit her so well. Her last name fit her so very well, in the same manner that it fit Lyon Measle so very well as a first name. They had, thanks to her last and his first name, an unspeakable, primitive and animalistic bond of sorts. A powerful, brave, courageous, strong, fearless, and ferocious Lion is easy to think of when reading this infamous "Lyon" surname. Yet, its spelling with a 'y' made one feel like something wasn't quite right. Which in turn and rightfully so, warned any addressors that something wasn't going to be quite right with these two animals. It was something that smelled like an air of fraudulence. Insincerity, perhaps. Which totally undermined all of the admirable lionesque traits.

After arriving, and parking at a perfect distance in the middle of the drive-in movie theater, Lyon and Kaizen pulled out the meals they had bought on the way over to the spectacle. A cheesy, ketchup topped hot dog and a burrito bowl with black beans, soy-based meat, coriander, an undisclosed type of red chilli powder, and a lot of guacamole. Respectively, of course. After devouring their meals, they seemed to attentively watch the film in silence. Lyon, however, could not stop looking at his watch the entire duration of the film. He felt a metaphorical clock clicking inside his head. The longer he took to go back to Bleu Moon, the longer it would take to disperse these bits of information he had obtained from Kaizen onto the Bleu Moon boys & girls, and the more likely it would be that he would forget exactly how to elaborate what Kaizen truly felt about Rylie and Yerma. So, as soon as the film ended, Lyon took a sip of his diet coke and floored the gas pedal as much as he could on his way back to Bleu Moon. Kaizen sipped on some of his parsley tea while listening to a classic arena rock playlist that Lyon had put together. It was very amusing, for Kaizen, to see a weasel scurry like a hamster inside its hamster ball.

Once they had arrived at Bleu Moon, Lyon and Kaizen partook in a quick dialogue on their way over to the door.

"Thanks for not killing my vibe bitchacho", Kaizen smugly said.

"Thank you for not killing mine", Lyon replied.

Kaizen quickly entered the door as soon as Lyon opened it, then helped himself to some chickpea tortilla chips, sat down on the sofa and turned on the tv.

As soon as Kaizen sat down and turned on the TV, Lyon knew where he stood in the eyes of Kaizen. Lyon was nothing but a vermin. Perhaps he didn't stink as much as Fagan, but still a vermin nonetheless. Lyon couldn't stand how little he felt next to Kaizen. Deep inside his core, Lyon blamed Kaizen for stirring up such feelings, when in reality, Lyon should have been blaming himself for not being a better individual. The world just was not built for lazy little Lyons to thrive. Oddly enough, Lyon somehow found pleasure from this self-degradation thought process going on inside his head. His mind wandered into the idea of having Fagan sodomize him. The best thing Lyon could do now to fulfill this fantasy, was to fulfill his agreement with the Bleu Moon girls. So, Lyon dismissed himself from Kaizen's presence, went to the Bleu Moon boys & girls' secret lair, which was Chap's much larger version of Lyon's white box on wheels, and disclosed the mini interview he had with Kaizen.

To Lyon's surprise, Yerma and Rylie did not respond the way he thought they would. "Disappointment!?", Rylie yelled. "Insecure?!", Yerma exclaimed. They quickly plotted their entrance back into Bleu Moon and scurried back there. When Kaizen saw Lyon, Chap, Fagan, Yerma, Gair, and Rylie walking through the door, with the house speaker on full blast, he prepared himself to go to bed. It was pretty much bedtime. He was, however, quickly cornered in the kitchen by everyone, disallowing him from going to sleep. There he stood, politely, waiting for the song to be over and for Fagan and Rylie to stop twerking the floor. It seemed like forever. Fagan and Rylie's buttcheeks went... WAP... WAP... WAP... on the floor. Or so they thought. It was more like little puppies wiping their butts on the floor. The worst part was that Chap recorded this entire event. Perhaps to somehow increase Fagan and Rylie's social status, making it seem like Kaizen was there for it, when in reality, he just wanted to go to bed. Just when Kaizen thought the song was over, Yerma stepped in front of him and shook her pajama-covered ass in front of him. This made Kaizen extremely uncomfortable and left everyone confused when he went back to bed unfazed. They all must have expected Kaizen to jump in and slap butts left and right, but when this clearly didn't happen, they also headed to their rooms. Just, rather confused.

That evening, inside Lyon's room, Lyon could be found with his phone and his cardboard covered wide-ruled composition notebook. The length of ClickClock videos he watched that night averaged a length of about twenty seconds. His notebook entry read...

11-16-2020

The kungflu virus vaccine is found to be 95.4% effective in clinical trial!

Who does Kaizen Domina think he is?!
WHAT DOES Kaizen Domina possess?!
Where the fuck did Kaizen Domina come from?!
When will I ever possess Kaizen Domina's level of audacity?!
Why does everyone and their mom seem to want Kaizen Domina?!
How many days are there until the next holiday break?!
Which witch witched & whose whom?!

An Intelligent Fruitcake

On the Seventeenth November evening of the year Two Thousand & Twenty... The Bleu Moon boys & girls could not entirely wrap their head around what had happened last night. In their eyes, and in the eyes of the individuals that stared back at them in the mirror before getting down and dirty day after day, anything other than hot stuff to describe themselves would be fallacious. But somehow, Kaizen, whom pretty much everyone (mostly the girls) desired with such a passion, made the reflections of themselves much clearer. It was as if someone had finally sprayed some lemon and mint cleaning spray on their mirrors and gracefully cleaned it with a reusable cotton paper towel. Their mirrors now communicated a much different message.

This message, was rather clear. Not one Bleu Moon member, aside from Kaizen of course, was anything greater than average. This sparked plugs inside each and every one of the Bleu Moon boys & girls. They wanted to be the very best at anything and everything, and secretly hated each other anytime that they cast a shadow on each other's abilities. The problem here was, Kaizen didn't want to be part of that. So Gair, who somehow had the most difficulty processing this public display of aversion by Kaizen (it reminded her too much of his similar private display of aversion towards her that summer), gathered everyone for a quick meeting inside her room via a quick super secret group instant message. Kaizen's evening classes were sure to keep him from coming upstairs and accidentally bump into their premeditated malfeasance.

Yerma had, in such an 'UnYerma Like Fashion', prepared a fruitcake for everyone to enjoy while they schemed. This fruitcake seemed ordinary, except it was made of gluten-free all purpose baking flour. It was also topped with some cherries, pineapple and walnuts. Not cashews, however. Goodness gracious forbid that she accidently give herself an allergic reaction during such an important meeting in such typical Yerma fashion. For this meeting had one goal only, and it wasn't to attend to Yerma's allergies. This meeting's goal was to figure out what should be done about Kaizen's public display of aversion.

After all, everyone seemed to be having enough of him. They all wanted to kill him. Especially Fagan, Rylie and Yerma. They thought that humping the floor would be a total rebellious act towards Kaizen, and in turn, would somehow trigger some sort of attraction that would want to chase them. Even Fagan desired this in spite of knowing Kaizen was a straight shooter through and through. Kaizen reminded Fagan of everything he wasn't... a Straight, Tall, Dark, Handsome & Virile Man. Kaizen reminded Yerma and Rylie of all of their shortcomings. Rylie could not forget how she fell short of coming into ahold of Kaizen's attention when he had toyed with her during 'The Hawt Seat' game or when she had rubbed her butt cheeks on his crotch in such an inappropriate time without the response she so desired. Yerma could not forget how she fell short of coming into a hold of Kaizen's lips when she had desired them to come closer and land on her cheeks during Gair's birthday gathering. To Kaizen, Yerma and Rylie were basically the same person. Just different cheeks.

You see, Rylie was the type that grabs another person to follow her 'smacking butt cheeks to floor' lead in hopes of sprinkling a bit of dissimulation to her mating call. This was seen last night when Lyon had told everyone how disappointed Kaizen felt for Rylie, which caused her to hump the floor hysterically while making sure Fagan had accompanied her act. This way, if word ever got out that she humped the floor in hopes of attracting Kaizen's attention, she could say she was 'just having fun' with Fagan. Yerma, on the other hand, did not like to dilly dally. She had taken Kaizen's comments about her insecurity and quickly devised her own 'baby got back' choreography right after Rylie and Fagan had finished dancing with the star watching them.

Little did they know, Kaizen was not the type whose mind wanders off of the chessboard. Gair could not handle rejection very well, Yerma's insecurities always brought out the worst in her, Rylie's constant disappointingly inappropriate demeanor would not get her very far in life, Fagan lived a starkly different lifestyle than Kaizen, Chap did not like being a closeted straight man, and Lyon had an utmost desire for Kaizen's status in life. This had been very clear to Kaizen for quite some time. His mere presence reminded them of everything that they were not. And they despised him because of it.

The one most incited by hate was obviously Lyon. The reasoning behind his hatred, aside from the self-evident envy, was quite simple. He had been the one that took time out to investigate Kaizen. This was a dead-end career that Lyon wanted to pursue after graduation. But here, he received no reward for his labor. He did the dirty work like a dog, yet, no bones were thrown his way. Instead, he witnessed the Bleu Moon girls become even more aroused by Kaizen's rejection. He wanted this kind of desire to be sparked inside of Fagan, yet the Bleu Moon girls had done nothing to further the promised payoff for his labor. None of the girls had even begun to urge Fagan to fulfill what had been promised to Lyon.

All of this dismissiveness would trigger some sort of intelligent psychopathic plan stemming from his neurosis. To the group that night, he said "All right everyone. It is quite clear that Kaizen is so very full of himself, and he deserves to be taught a lesson. I know that he has the hots for Yerma or Ruth Leslie, one of the two. It just cannot be that a man walks away like that at the sight of these two, ya know? He needs to receive some sort of punishment. He should know that dismissing another individual's presence is not okay at all! We have done nothing wrong to deserve this! This can lead us... I mean... you know... people in general that are affected by this, to do some very bad things..." Lyon's scheme with the rest of the Bleu Moon boys and girls this night was quite brief, but sufficient enough to prepare them for the week before thanksgiving break.

This evening, inside Lyon's room, Lyon could be found with his phone and his cardboard covered wide-ruled composition notebook. The length of ClickClock videos he watched that night averaged a length of about fifteen seconds. His notebook entry read...

11-17-2020

Dr. Pho Tucci, the Chief Medical Advisor to the President, discusses kungflu symptoms!

Who discusses kungflu symptoms with Pho
Tucci?!
WHAT DOES KAIZEN Domina possess?!
Where would Kaizen's weakness be?!
When will Kaizen get what he deserves?!
Why is Kaizen so narcissistic?!
How can one move an immovable force?!
Which witch witched & whose whom?!

Derealization

On the Twenty-First November day of the year Two Thousand & Twenty... The attempted gaslighting began. The Bleu Moon boys & girls wanted to redeem themselves from the embarrassing intimate scene displayed on the kitchen floor about four days ago. They wanted to redeem themselves in a way that didn't make it seem like the problem was them, but rather, Kaizen Domina. They wanted to bestow all responsibility upon his shoulders, as if he was the one that caused them to hump the floor that night. They wanted to do all of this while saving face and without seeming confrontational all the while making it seem like they were positioned at a higher social ranking than Kaizen Domina.

This was quite the task. Kaizen Domina was not someone one could easily manipulate into questioning their own sanity. He saw things as they were. This made it even harder for the Bleu Moon boys and girls to place him in a vulnerable position of self-doubt and self-unawareness. Per the Bleu Moon boys & girls' agenda, Lyon messaged the Bleu Moon group that Kaizen was a part of with the following message...

"For our cornhole game tonight, everyone will exhibit themselves on their way to the gaming platform. And in order to give everyone the entrance that they deserve, message back with the following information to prepare your introductions...

Your full name:

Your height:

Your weight:

Your hometown:

Your nickname:

Your birth city:

Your pet's name:

Your favorite number:

Your mother's maiden name:

Your high school's name:

Your favorite food:

Your preferred intro song:"

This fake display of rapport would do many things for the Bleu Moon boys & girls. On the one hand, should Kaizen decide not to respond to any of the prompts, it would give them an excuse to backlash and badmouth Kaizen as they could take this to mean that Kaizen hated them or whatever blown out of proportion story they could come up with. On the other hand, should Kaizen decide to respond to these prompts, it would seem as if he was the one wanting to be part of their friendly celebrations. It would seem as if he didn't feel extremely uncomfortable trying to make his way back to his bed that night when Yerma, Rylie and Fagan were shaking their asses on the floor. Kaizen was, quite clearly, forced to submit his responses to these prompts. Unfortunately for Bleu Moon, Kaizen did not respond very seriously to any of the prompts.

This was unfortunate for the Bleu Moon boys and girls as it would make the path to their ultimate goal much longer and more tedious. You see, this wasn't just any 'spontaneous' celebration that came out of thin air. Lyon, given his descendance from Becker Measle and Carey Measle, knew the best way to get revenge on their undesirable individuals. He had quite the role models indeed. Becker & Carey Measle thrived on their clients' intimate information. Especially Carey. She had instilled inside of Lyon all of her cunning ways. She would always tell her son growing up... *Money is not the hottest commodity there is my son. Information is. So always remember to get as much information from everyone as possible, my son. You may become a hot commodity someday because of it. And don't forget... Be Kind... Be Smart... Be Special.* Carey Measle would not only get typical vital information from her clients such as their birthdate, but she would often go out of her way to attend her clients' events herself in hopes of knowing other vital information of celebrated guests. Once in a while, she would stumble upon just enough information to successfully log into a clients' bank account and transfer an unsuspicious amount of money to her bank account during peak activity. Becker Measle always eased Carey by reassuring her that if she *reasons the memo of the transfer to be a 'TIP', most of these clients' accountants won't even give it too much mind. These people are loaded and the accountants merely want to prepare financial statements and move on to the next client.* Becker Measle wasn't wrong, most of their clients made so much revenue that they wouldn't bat an eye at Lyon's next surprise present. What a twisted habit they had given Lyon. *All in a good day's work* they always told him before giving him his presents.

Lyon's hard work did not pay off. His setup did not weaken Kaizen in the least. No important information was given out. He responded to such prompts in the same manner that he had walked past the kitchen full of humping bonobos four nights ago. Unfazed, unbothered, and seemingly unattentive.

Kaizen's nonchalantness triggered Lyon, after all, he was doing the Bleu Moon boys & girls' dirty work to no avail. Lyon was beginning to become accustomed to Kaizen's subdued cockiness. It was as if Kaizen always knew what would happen in the future, given how well prepared he always seemed to tackle any obstacle. To Lyon at this point, Kaizen was either clairvoyant or had a very well commissioned guardian angel. Lyon thought there was no way any normal being could resist an invitation to connect with other desirable human beings as much as Kaizen had been able to do. Lyon would eventually have to resort to more tyrannical means if he was ever to attain vulnerable information from Kaizen.

Given that Kaizen had called Bleu Moon's bluff, everyone had to commit to playing cornhole that night. It would be unbecoming to go through all of this trouble to get Kaizen to join them for a game of cornhole and then decide not to go through with their event. It would give Kaizen every excuse to not respond to any further invitations from them. It would give Kaizen exactly what he wanted. It would give Kaizen the most desirable thing in the world. It would give Kaizen peace of mind.

The Bleu Moon boys and girls could not give Kaizen the luxury of peace of mind. They needed to drain him of his energy. So they ordered a few pizzas, as if refuting Kaizen's mockingly response to the favorite food prompt. They put on low quality television in the form of an 'internet flicks' series and even invited Patsy Chi over so she could watch Kaizen's demise. Among the Bleu Moon members not playing cornhole that night was Fagan. He could not stand all of the attention that was being placed on

Kaizen. So he soliloquized his way on out of the cornhole competition in true Fagan fashion. Yerma could be found nowhere near the Bleu Moon backyard because she was too busy wiping butt that night. Aside from Patsy Chi, there was another guest appearance that night, which could be found in the form of a very attractive young lady watching from behind the window next door. If one squinted hard enough, one could make a lovely silhouette snacking on what appeared to be chickpea tortilla chips. Radisson Quebec sure did know how to take care of her figure.

Kaizen knew a lovely lady was watching, and he didn't mind exhibiting his abilities in front of a lovely crowd of one, but he wanted out of this as quickly as possible, so, he had already decided he would lose his first game on purpose. Chap took care of organizing the brackets. Lyon made the intros of every cornhole matchup via a megaphone. He ensured that he praised himself more so than he did others that evening, so as to somehow display his superiority. Everybody else focused on their gameplay. They would have brackets keeping track of the status of who won and who lost, with each match being a game to twenty-one points. The first round matchups were Chap versus Kaizen, Lyon versus Rylie, and Patsy versus Gair. Chap, being the one that practiced the most cornhole out of everyone, expected to win. And win he did. In fact, he had won so quickly the outcome smelled fishier than Rylie's undergarments. That didn't keep her from beating Lyon however. He was not much of a competition really. It was tedious however. Their game took so long and made everyone quite exhausted. Gair had already agreed to make Patsy look good in front of Kaizen in hopes of finding him a new distraction. Perhaps Kaizen was into competitive and unrefined girls like Patsy. He wasn't. Kaizen's amorous attention was placed somewhere next door. In hopes of tiring Kaizen out, Chap had made a loser bracket which consisted of Kaizen and Gair. Chap had excused Lyon out of the game, claiming that he just looked so tired. He was not wrong as Lyon always looked tired. But after his matchup with Rylie, he looked even more so than usual. His cystic acne looked worse. Those lumps on his face looked more explosive than ever. Just not as explosive as Kaizen's quick rise to the top of the bracket. Kaizen defeated Gair, and then continued to defeat Patsy. After seeing that the Bleu Moon's agenda was to tire him out as much as possible, he could not help himself but play like he typically does, almost as if telling them they needed to do better if they hoped to leave him panting and wheezing like Lyon Measle. Chap defeated Rylie just as easily as Kaizen had defeated Gair and Patsy. Chap, being the closeted straight sexist of the group, expected Kaizen to win. But he did not expect him to win as quickly as he had done so. So when it came to Kaizen and Chap's matchup, it was a total surprise when they had both arrived at eighteen points each, and Kaizen went on to finish the game by scoring a cornhole on him.

Kaizen had never, ever played cornhole in his life before that night. He was, however, the most prepared, athletic and strategic individual the world had ever known. He could easily adapt and overcome any challenge thrown at him if he truly desired to do so. The Bleu Moon boys and girls were just not even close to being of the same caliber as Kaizen. Patsy excused herself to go back home to do, for the same reason, what Radisson Quebec would end up doing that night. After Kaizen had won the mini cornhole tournament that night, he celebrated by slapping his chest and proceeding to point to the window next door while mouthing the words... "That was for you, Red Raddy". Radisson could be found later that night in her bathtub, flicking the bean like a disc jockey whilst reminiscing about Kaizen. Lyon Measle had struggled trying to feed three birds with one scone. Meanwhile, without even trying, Kaizen seemed to be quite adept at entertaining multiple bitches with one bone. All in a good day's work.

That evening, inside Lyon's room, Lyon could be found with his phone and his cardboard covered wide-ruled composition notebook. The

length of ClickClock videos he watched that
night averaged a length of about ten seconds. His
notebook entry read...

11-21-2020

Disease Control Center revises Travel Health
Notice system for kungflu!

Who remains sedentary yet athletic?!
WHAT DOES KAIZEN DOMINA possess?!
Where does Kaizen come from?!
When will my acne go away?!
Why won't my acne go away?!
How does acne form?!
Which witch witched & whose whom?!

Breaking Ruse! A Lying Weasel

On the Third December morning of the year Two
Thousand & Twenty... a little over a week had
passed since the Bleu Moon boys & girls had
unsuccessfully attempted to embarrass Kaizen.
Lyon was the most devastated by the outcome. As
each day passed, he had pondered ways in which
he could gather just a tiny ounce of dirt on
Kaizen. Anything would do. These are the
struggles of an extroverted idiot who tries to pick
on an imperturbable individual. Lucky for Lyon,
that morning he received a phishing email. This
sparked an idea that would redeem his fruitcake
covered plan.

   During lunch, he made his way over to
Kaizen's room, without even bothering to knock.
"Can I borrow your laptop", he asked. "What
for?", Kaizen replied. "Well, if you must know,
I've just received an email saying I've been
hacked", Lyon quickly replied with a fluctuating
voice that communicated as much despair as he
could muster up, in hopes of making this scene a
convincing plausibility. Bullshit. That is what it
was. But still, Kaizen didn't mind letting Lyon
make a fool of himself once more. While Kaizen
was munching on his chickpea snacks, Lyon was

using Kaizen's desk, chair and laptop while making his best attempt to cover the screen from Kaizen's viewing angle.

It was a bummer for Lyon, as he had found absolutely nothing about Kaizen. His internal storage was empty. It still read that it had over two-hundred gigabytes of storage. What was most odd of all was that there were literally no applications installed on his laptop except one. Who would've thought the only application on Kaizen's work laptop only included a web browsing app. To Lyon, this was foreign, perhaps even alien sorcery. Sure, he was able to access his email as he was supposedly there to do so, but his ultimate goal remained unsatisfied. Lyon could now either choose to leave and call it quits on his nosy reporter venture, or find a way to stall the situation in order to get the information he had wanted. When it came to making himself look like a fool, Lyon never seemed to give up.

When Lyon had used Kaizen's business card, he had spent a significant amount of money on independent triple x rated DVDs. How pathetic could one be? What had made this decision extra pathetic, aside from the fact that he was still a DVD user, is the fact that all of the funds he had used could have been put to better use by compensating someone from Las Begass to give him that adult entertainment he craved. Was Lyon not aware that these transactions show up on bank statements? More than two decades on planet earth and he still did not seem to have an ounce of financial literacy.

Most of Lyon's actions would resonate with those of a little boy. This being possible from someone that had the body of a full grown adult male, was quite the mind numbing puzzle. No greater example of Lyon acting like a hopeless little boy could be made than when he had tried to belittle Kaizen's advertising agency. That statement would be similar to someone on the corner of a light stop screaming at an off road pickup truck owner "One day, I'll have one bigger than yours! And it'll be diesel!". What kind of idiot would go out of their way to do that?

Lyon's conniving ways did not seem to have an end. His desires to have at least an inch of gossip to disperse with somebody else were just too great. He would, eventually, have something to gossip about. It just would not be obtained now, and he would not be able to indulge in such gossip just yet. Especially inside of Bleu Moon. Lyon started to become less at ease as time went on. He no longer indulged in Click Clock as much as he used to.

Given Lyon's nature, he of course, refused to give up on finding at least a little bit of dirt during Kaizen's hours-long lunch break on this sunny Tuesday. He went over to Kaizen and grabbed his phone right out of his hand. "I need to call my father so that he can help me with this situation" Lyon said as he made his way outside of the house using the side porch and heading into the backyard. As he made his way over to the bench by the fire pit, Lyon called Chap, in order to fulfill what they had planned.

The Bleu Moon boys and girls were desperate. They HAD to get ahold of something that could potentially place Kaizen in a vulnerable spot. Lyon seemed to be on the right track to redemption as he called Chap, "Alright Chap, can you try to log into Kaizen's Pinstabook account. I have his phone, so we have everything we need", Lyon demanded. "Ah yes of course, give me literally a second while I open up a new tab", Chap replied. "Awesome. I have his email ready, his Pinstabook account says it's redraddyrocks@email.com", Lyon informed. "Okay, I'm using that email and now I'm clicking on the I forgot my password notification. Did you get that email notification yet", Chap questioned. "Okay yes, I am letting the system know that this was indeed Kaizen trying to log in. Are you in?", Lyon asked. "I'm in", Chap assured. "Okay, perfect. Stay logged in. Gotta go. Bye, love ya", Lyon uttered.

All of this conversation was being observed, but not heard, by Kaizen from Lyon's room. As soon as he saw Lyon coming back to the house, he quickly made his way outside of Lyon's room, realized he almost left his chickpeas there, came back, and sprinted back again towards his room quicker than a ninja. "Thank you for letting me borrow your phone", Lyon said as he returned the stolen device to Kaizen. What made this situation extremely amusing was that Lyon acted as if he had not just tyrannically forced his will. It was as if he wasn't aware that he had neither asked to borrow Kaizen's phone and he also had not waited for a "No problem" or an "Of course" or perhaps even a "You're welcome" from Kaizen. Lyon sure did overestimate Kaizen's gullibility.

That Tuesday evening, inside Lyon's room, Lyon could be found with his phone and his cardboard covered wide-ruled composition notebook. The length of ClickClock videos he watched that night averaged a length of about five seconds. His notebook entry read...

12-3-2020

The Committee Advising on Immunization Processes recommends that healthcare professionals and older people living in long-term care facilities be offered a vaccine first in the initial phases of the kungflu vaccination program

Who is considered 'older people'?!
WHAT DOES KAIZEN DOMINA POSSESS?!
Where do pornstars get their sildenafil?!

When will my penis ever go boom-boom with
another penis?!
Why is my penis so small?!
How can I become a gay pornstar?!
Which witch witched & whose whom?!

Game Is Afoot

On the Eleventh December evening of the year Two Thousand & Twenty... "Come, Fagan, come! The game is afoot. Not a word! Into your clothes and come!", Lyon whispered into Fagan's little room. *A man who takes charge*, Fagan thought. *Me likey likey*, Fagan thought some more. So he did just that. He came into his clothes and followed suit.

This evening, they wandered 'The Hogain' neighborhood. Blending in was easy as there were a lot of stupid adolescent individuals drifting from a kickback at one house to a kickback at another house. Gorgonzola College's pupils, especially the boys, found the neighborhood quite promising. The ultimate goal of these boys was to 'gain some hoes', if you will. Quite healthy endeavors if most were to ask most. These endeavors, however, were not shared by Lyon on this brief night.

"I was able to get ahold of Kaizen's Pinstabook account, but I believe he's beginning to smell what we're stepping in. Does thou catcheth my drifteth?", Lyon questioned.

"Oh, I catcheth thy drifteth alright. Sooo... what now?", Fagan inquired back.

"Well, Lou Guinea's family was not able to take care of Kaizen's family members back home. I think this will have to be like the time we were able to get those country hicks that call themselves law enforcement to shoot that cheerleading Bobby Gaits in the head. Glad they haven't enforced those hicks to wear body cameras yet or we'd be in so much trouble. I can't believe Bobby ended up surviving. Man oh man he definitely can't think straight anymore, hahaha. I think it's best if we take matters into our own hands this time around, ya dig?"

"Quite barbaric. Can't say that I likey likey."

"You've never complained about my methods before"

"I'm not complaining"

"You're not? What does thou calleth this?"

"I never complain! How Am I complaining?! When do I ever complain about you jerking it at three in the morning, or your face cysts, your general lack of nutritional awareness, or the fact that you steal my clothes?!"

"Okay good, so it's a done deal. You stand guard in the kitchen and I'll choke him out and we can hang him by a river or slough or something. Everyone's busy anyways, with it being finals week and all. It'd be easy to make it look like a suicide. It shouldn't be hard to find a noose around here, ya know?"

"Does your depravity know no bounds"

"Nope. Okay let's go!"

This had not been the first time Lyon and Fagan had tried to hurt Kaizen or his family. From the first moment they had moved in together, Lyon and Fagan did not like Kaizen. They despised how very charming everyone thought he was. So they had resorted to getting help from one of Gorgonzola's finest basketball team members. He went by the name of Lou Guinea, a ginormous forward donning a pussy tickler in between his mouth and nose. Lou Guinea's father and his relative, Matt & John were good pals with Fagan's father. They were part of the very dishonorable industry known as insurance. They had used insurance information to track down information on Kaizen's family member's vehicles and then had someone try to crash into them. This was done unsuccessfully, leaving Lyon and Fagan hungry for finishing an unfinished job.

Fagan and Lyon's prying nature was hard to satiate. They wanted to pry and pry, like a couple of ill-fated detectives. It was until after the fact of performing ill-fated actions, such as forcibly attaining personal information about Kaizen, that Lyon realized just how ungraceful his modus operandi really was. The disgusting part about tonight's manifestation of Lyon's modus operandi was that he wanted to perform the same ungodly acts on Kaizen's dead body that were performed on him during his high school years. He just had to find a way to somehow turn him lifeless. He just didn't know whether it should be him performing those ungodly acts on Kaizen or if there was a way that Kaizen could help him emulate those same high school acts that were performed on him. Only Lyon's depravity could even imagine such things so swiftly.

The first step to actually fulfilling such twisted desires, was to place Kaizen in a vulnerable enough position where he could be killed off. Perhaps, not much needed to be done. It could be that Kaizen was already in such a vulnerable position, back at Bleu Moon. Lyon had always underestimated Kaizen in every regard. More so than any of the other Bleu Moon members. It was this horrible lack of discernment that would put him in a state he has never been before. A state that very few ever go to, confidently, and return with that same intact confident aura.

Back at Bleu Moon, Kaizen was doing what he usually does. Sipping on some tea while reading his latest enjoyable read. He liked reading himself to sleep, after all, he was weeks ahead in many of his classes. His room's light, although in the basement, could be seen from outside of the south street of Bleu Moon.

It was this street, Besmut Avenue, from where the irascible Lyon and his Fagan were arriving. "Watch this Fagan!" exclaimed Lyon as he made his way over to the western side of the house where the light radiating from Kaizen's room could also be seen. Lyon unzipped his jeans, pulled out his little 'legume', and started urinating on Kaizen's windows. "Don't get too excited!", he yelled at Fagan. "Shut up and do what you came here to do", said Fagan. So after a few quick piss streams from Lyon splattered onto the basement window, they made their way inside, knowing that no one would be making their way into the house. Still, this didn't stop them from locking the house doors just in case unwanted eyes wandered into the house.

Kaizen knew that there was no dog urinating on the window. He could tell by the sound of the stream. Most healthy dogs have a steady sounding stream with at least some pressure behind it. This stream sounded like someone had spit a few times after they had brushed their teeth. A foreign concept to Lyon. As the aspirant dog came downstairs, Kaizen knew something had to be done. Soon after Lyon stepped foot on the basement's carpet, Fagan quickly rushed past him to get his coffee mug. Kaizen took this moment to summon the well deserved act of shoving Lyon into the wall. Fagan heard the commotion and pusillanimously ran back upstairs. Lyon tackled Kaizen's torso with a force that ended up ramming Kaizen back into his well lit room. They landed on Kaizen's bed, causing the wooden bed base to break.

Kaizen's torso was now pinned in between the bed and Lyon's shoulder, whereas Lyon's head was pinned in between Kaizen's left arm and torso. From the moment Lyon had tackled Kaizen onto his bed, one thing was quite evident. The odds of this duel were never in the favor of the least prepared individual.

Elementary

With the entirety of his weight being projected onto the shoulder pinning Kaizen's torso, Lyon completely believed physics was on his side. Maybe he should have also added a few common sense books into his repertoire, as his neck was still in the cusp of Kaizen's elbow and in turn, at Kaizen's will. With Kaizen keeping his hands locked underneath Lyon's left armpit, all he had to do was flex his well toned bicep once in a while to let the animal know who was in charge here. What was astounding about this duel was how much more weight Lyon had on his side, yet, he could not find any way to leverage it. Perhaps he should've laid off the steak so that cordwainers don't have to struggle so much when sourcing their shoe making material.

Kaizen was a middleweight and Lyon almost reached heavyweight status, so any way you'd like to put it, this was clearly not a fair match. For whom it was unfair, at first sight, could be a little trickier to see. But the picture was there, clear as day, one would just have to focus in a bit more. The more Lyon tried to squirm, the more he risked decreasing the blood flow to his T-Rex like brain. If Lyon tried to scream to

Fagan for help, he knew he would look even more of an imbecile. He truly was at the mercy of Kaizen.

For Kaizen, an undisclosed olympic martial artist, Lyon was no match. While fighting upright, that is. Kaizen had never participated in any ground grappling disciplines before. But Kaizen was able to analyze the situation mid flight to his bed. He knew two things for certain about Lyon, which was that he was stubborn, exercised a lot, and ate a lot of meat. Okay that was three things, but still. That was the equation to an inevitable downfall against a vegan Kaizen. Perhaps Lyon didn't analyze the situation very well, but he could now feel that Kaizen was a well oiled machine. Kaizen could have chosen to end him right then and there or he could have chosen to let Lyon live to fight another day.

"From a utilitarian perspective, Lyon was very lucky. You see, Kaizen knew that it was more embarrassing for anyone to have experienced this situation of trying to finish off someone one spites so much only to be shown just how miniscule one really is. Kaizen had made the decision of giving Lyon purgatory in the flesh. But not before toying with him a little bit first.

"Whaddup little bitch. You like that?", Kaizen questioned.

"Hrrk", was the best sound Lyon could produce in such a position.

Feeling that Lyon was about to pass out, Kaizen maneuvered out of the bed in hopes of standing upright in order to drag Lyon out of his room. Just as he was standing up, Lyon began to squirm again, so, without losing grip of Lyon, Kaizen jumped over him and landed on the bed facing upwards. As he did so, Lyon's body followed suit all the while Kaizen had tucked his knees inwards, ensuring that they would meet Lyon's back as it landed on them. Lyon's arms were now being hooked by Kaizen's hands while Lyon's back rested on Kaizen's sharp knees. "How's the view from up there?... Bitch", Kaizen asked.

Lyon's vitamin deficiency from his poor diet, which made his body focus more on the constant tingling sensations in his extremities, didn't allow him to experience as much of the pain from what was occurring inside his body. The cartilage from his ribcage began to tear as Kaizen kept pulling on his arms. Lyon's adrenaline also made this pain feel much less painful than it actually was. Eventually, his arms began to give up and straightened into a crucifixion position. "It's great actually. I'm really enjoying this. Haaaaaaawk tuah!", he replied to Kaizen while attempting to seem like he was unaffected by the very vulnerable position Kaizen had placed him in.

Lyon was just so pathetic at this point. He caused so much disgust to Kaizen, that Kaizen couldn't help but move his feet, one by one, into the position where his knees had been, essentially in a leg pressing position now, so that he could propel Lyon's body in the direction of the door. Once Lyon had begun to stand up and finish the fight he had instigated, Kaizen was already waiting for him in the most calm and assured orthodox fighting stance possible. Lyon didn't know what to do, so he mimicked Kaizen's fighting stance and assumed an orthodox fighting position as well.

This fight would be a piece of cake. For Kaizen. He did a shoulder feint, causing Lyon to move back closer to the door into a southpaw position while using his hands to cover the front side of his body. Kaizen used this split second to roundhouse the popliteal region of Lyon's right leg with his front left leg in the swiftest motion Lyon had ever seen. It was as if lightning had just struck Lyon's right leg. The acceleration of Kaizen was unmatched. Lyon tried his best to remain calm in an attempt to hide his pain from Kaizen. But all this really meant, was that the little dog had frozen. Lyon emulated a similar expression to that of a rat when it comes into contact with a never before experienced stimulus. A frozen expression of helplessness. Kaizen had already met this expression several times and had actually come to expect it out of anyone that tried to challenge him. Getting this expression out of his opponents was nothing complex for Kaizen. It was elementary.

Kraka-Boom! Another round-kick to Lyon's right leg. Lyon remained frozen. Kraka-boom! Another round-kick to Lyon's right leg. Lyon began to limp as he walked backwards heading for the stairs. "Okay, I was just kidding around man", Lyon told Kaizen. "Come back when you're not drunk!", Kaizen said, knowing Lyon wasn't drunk. But it would be amusing for Kaizen to see Lyon's expression to this comment. Kaizen knew that Lyon would think, *Oh my goodness! He thinks I'm drunk. This is perfect. I can leave and save face.* So he did leave, running back upstairs to Fagan like a coward. Fagan and Lyon headed back out to the Hogain that night.

"What happened back there?", Fagan asked.

"Nothing. Let's just say we're going to have to pull out the big guns if we want Kaizen to break.", Lyon replied.

"You mean it's time to bring out the Sidwells?"

"You read my mind. We can't really pull the same stunt we did with Bobby Gaits because, well, Bleu Moon's just too close to the school and that highly trafficked coffee shop."

"Do you think they'll be up for the task?"

"Perhaps not now, but after winter break I reckon they will. I don't know why you're asking me, you know them better."

"You're right. And I also 'RECKON' they will too. God! I'm so glad we've moved on from that Shakespearean language you pulled out of your ass earlier. Has anybody told you that you talk funny when you're nervous?"

"I don't talk funny and I'm not nervous. Stop with your hallucinations and let's go make our presence known at whatever Hogain is hosting tonight."

This was quite the socialist strategy Lyon had conjured up. It seemed effective. All they had to do now was make an appearance at a few gatherings within the Hogain to have a solid alibi should Kaizen ever decide to speak out about what had happened tonight at Bleu Moon. It would also be a shame if somehow someone else had been watching this entire incident as well, and perhaps eventually decided to write about it and spread it to the masses. Lyon and Fagan had a lot of risk mitigating to do tonight. The more they made their presence known that night, the more they lowered the probability anyone would ever find out about their failed attempted murder that night. After ensuring the other Bleu Moon members also patrolling Hogain had arrived back home that night, Lyon and Fagan decided to head back home. No one from Gorgonzola College or anywhere else would ever believe Kaizen should he try to expose Lyon and Fagan. Or would they? This was the question that ran inside of Lyon's mind that night while laying in his bed. The length of ClickClock videos he watched that night averaged a length of about zero seconds, for he had not even bothered to pick up his phone nor his cardboard covered wide-ruled composition notebook. He was too busy anguishing about the unsuccessful Eleventh December night he had just experienced. It was the most restless night he would ever experience.

The Great Patsy

On an evening occurring a couple of weeks after the Nineteenth January evening of the year Two Thousand & Twenty-One... Yerma could be found finishing heating up one of her meals she had prepared earlier that week. At this moment, she was attempting to clean all of the filth in the kitchen. This was quite a futile exercise. The best thing one could do would be to not make a mess in the first place. But Yerma was accustomed to the filth and disease, so she shrugged her shoulders and wiped the kitchen counters with the same amount of elbow grease that she wiped ass with. Kaizen on the other hand, did not appreciate filth nor disease, and he intended to do some deep cleaning fairly soon. He stumbled into the house that evening, weeping and crying. Kaizen knew those freshman year acting classes would eventually come in handy. The sight of Kaizen crying inevitably got Yerma worried. "I'm just one guy", Kaizen sobbed. "Do you need a hug?", Yerma asked without waiting for an answer and continued to hug him. She could feel him trembling. Just then, a rat came from the direction of the front door and ran past her foot as it made its way underneath the stove. Yerma jumped onto the kitchen counter and Kaizen's fighting instinct came out. Just after quickly wiping his tears, he pulled out the cabinet underneath the oven only to find the rat was not there. This was the second time a rat had pussilanimously left his presence. After their hug was interrupted by a rat, Yerma and Kaizen moved over to the living room and continued their conversation on the couch. They talked that night about how he felt hurt that Riley held no feelings for him. Yerma did her best in trying to comfort him, secretly hoping this conversation would eventually lead back upstairs into her room. It didn't. Kaizen did eventually go upstairs one night to talk to the Bleu Moon girls, pretending to blame himself for how so distant the Bleu Moon boys and girls had been acting after winter break. Kaizen was pretending like he cared about them in the same manner that they had pretended they cared about him. This made the house freeze in the same manner that Lyon had frozen when he received Kaizen's roundhouse kick. They didn't know how to fully respond to Kaizen's tears.

The return back to the school year from winter break had been odd for the Bleu Moon boys and girls. They were so accustomed to bumping into Kaizen watching films on television, but there was none of that this last semester. It made it extremely difficult for the plan they had conjured up over winter break to come to fruition. You see, they either wanted Senica Sidewell to drain Kaizen's energy by taking him to poundtown which would in turn leave him weak enough to finish him off and dispose of his body. Given that most of the nation was in lockdown, it would be difficult to trace back the crime back to them without violating the distancing laws set in place by the nation. They also had the backup plan of instigating a fight between Bozeman and Kaizen and using Rylie as the reasoning for the altercation. Both of these possibilites were very predictable plans stemming from the Bleu Moon boys and girls, as well as amateur ways of trying to complicate the life of another individual. Kaizen had already prepared his Bleu Moon escape plan during the winter break, as well as setting up a contingency which would cause any of their plans to go awry.

By now one should know Kaizen is not one to dilly dally. This should have been very clear to the Bleu Moon boys and girls, but somehow, they didn't seem to account for this. Since the beginning of this final school year, Kaizen already knew he was going to finish his coursework far before anyone else would. He only had classes on Tuesdays and Thursdays, so his homework sessions were swift, efficient and allowed him to finish all homework before the weekend and it even allowed him to get ahead on the big projects. So much so was the case, he had essentially finished all of the assignments that were to come up for the rest of the school year, and all he had to do was turn those assignments in on their due dates as the weeks went by. When the winter break ended, his mind was free from schoolwork distraction.

During winter break, Kaizen was able to log out of the external devices used by Lyon and Chap to hack into his Pinstabook account via brute force. Kaizen had also taken winter break as an opportunity to plant a seed. He knew Rylie had wanted to ride his dick during the entirety of his stay at Bleu Moon. He also knew that the Bleu Moon boys and girls wanted to destroy him in the most humiliating way possible. This meant he had to leave Bleu Moon as soon as possible, but not before beating the fuck out of the Bleu Moon boys and girls. Legally and psychologically of course. You beat filth-ridden teams like the Bleu Moon boys and girls with three things: distraction, diversion, and division. Then you put them on display for the whole world to see.

Kaizen sent a huge distraction over to Rylie in the form of a voice message. "Listen Riley, I feel very strongly about you. You're fun. You're beautiful. I've been trying to hold my feelings back about how I feel about you for quite some time now. If you feel the same way, then let me know and I'm sure there are a lot of places where you and I can go and spend some time alone together. I know quite a few places where we wouldn't have to wear masks. However, if you don't feel the same way then tear the bandage off already." Kaizen tried to sound like he was in so much pain trying to hold back feelings that were not there for Rylie. This was done right before Christmas, so it would place in her mind that he was thinking about her during the holidays. Quite the emotional oomph the situation needed. Kaizen had also sent a voice message in similar fashion to Gair, with the subject being focused on Kaizen and Rylie's 'friendship'. Kaizen had expressed hopes of not ruining the so called friendship Rylie thought they had, knowing this would make Rylie act distant in hopes of appearing mysterious to Kaizen. Kaizen was so thoughtful. Given Gair and Bleu Moon's divulging nature, Gair was bound to do Kaizen's sympathetic work for him. When Gair would tell Rylie about the conversation she had with Kaizen, it would appear as if he actually cared about Rylie. It was the toughest acting round Kaizen had ever been a part of, since the scum of Bleu Moon was anything but lovable. Having separation via a phone definitely helped him out, but given Kaizen's thespian skills, an in person act would have also been a very believable display of affection.

Rylie inevitably told the rest of the Bleu Moon boys and girls and they found this to be the perfect opportunity to somehow find a way to take advantage of Kaizen in order to kill him off. They had to be crafty however. Lyon and Fagan had already discussed dragging in the Sidwells to bring over some distraction of their own. But they didn't account for Kaizen's diversion. The rest of the last semester consisted of Kaizen leaving the Bleu Moon premises every time he was not on school conference calls. His business was a well oiled machine so there was no need to worry in that department. But any day that was not Tuesday or Thursday, he would go straight to the Uptown Mall located at 4750 N Multiplication St, Suntan, Warrington 66501. Inside this mall was his favorite physical bookstore, in which he could refine his escape plan. This habit would make it extremely difficult for Senica to bump into him and take him to poundtown. Poor Senica. Anytime Kaizen headed back to Bleu Moon, he also made a habit of locking his bedroom door. None of the Bleu Moon members ever knew he had set up a stealthy camera inside his room either. They were bound to eventually invade his privacy like they usually do and be caught on camera.

Rylie had even tried to bring Bozeman downstairs in hopes of bumping and instigating a fight between Kaizen and Bozeman, yet, the door was always locked so her and the rest of the Bleu Moon boys and girls' plans never quite made it to fruition. As if Bozeman even stood a chance in a fighting duel with Kaizen. Desperation got the best of everyone. They all wanted to bait Kaizen but none of them wanted to be the bait at this point. They had tried and failed time after time. As Valentine's day approached, they decided to bring The Great Patsy into play. Patsy Chi had been waiting for this moment for the longest time. She wanted to succeed at what no one seemed to pull off... fully grasping Kaizen's attention. The best plan the Bleu Moon boys and girls could come up with was for Patsy to write a tempting yet very formal sounding letter to Kaizen.

      "I'll love you more than you'll ever know" is what Patsy wanted to write in the valentine's day card intended for Kaizen. "Kaizen, it has been a lovely honor meeting you. - Patsy" is what she ended up writing instead. BINGO! Thought Kaizen. It was time for him to bring out L'Homme Fatale. He ended up writing a valentine's day letter back to her that read, "Patsy, thank you for being a part of my life. I wouldn't be where I'm at today without you. You are The Invisible Hand in my life." Kaizen being a romantic capitalist, expected Patsy to know he was referencing a key forefather of capitalism, as through her self-interest in deciding not to dorm with her 'friends', she eventually came to enrich the whole community, as if by an invisible hand. This community was Kaizen, as without her in the picture, there had been an open room inside a house close to Gorgonzola College for him to delve deep into academia quite efficiently. Unfortunately, this went over her head. She was only interested in bedding Kaizen at this point. She wanted to ensure he was really interested in her, so she wrote to him, this time via short message service, "Kaizen, I gave Valentine cards to everyone at Bleu Moon. It sounds like you're interested in me. What is it you like about me? Just so you know, I am not interested and you've been making me feel very uncomfortable."

Seeking to toy with her in the same manner Patsy intended to toy with Kaizen, he wrote back to her, "No Pats, at one point in time you did seem interesting, but lately you've been making me feel uncomfortable as well. A valentine's day card is not going to win me over. It was nice to meet you." Patsy was devastated. Infuriated actually, at how she had just been rejected by Kaizen. She also found out Kaizen had left valentine's cards with the other members at Bleu Moon as well. What a great diversion. She didn't want the conversation to end there, but she also didn't want to risk further embarrassment so she wrote a letter back to Kaizen and had one of the Bleu Moon members leave it in his door for him to run into after taking a shower. It read,

"The Valentine card was not to win you over. It was a friendly gesture. Good luck in life! - Pats"

Friendly gesture?... As if! Kaizen and Patsy had never had a one on one interaction ever. This was Patsy code for, "C'mon Kaizen, just say you want me so I can bend over and entrap you inside of me!" This whole interaction took place in the span of a couple of weeks within February. Kaizen spent the next few months playfully courting Patsy as if he was actually interested in her. These months of public display of affection towards Patsy by Kaizen ended up infuriating Rylie. Voila! The division portion of Kaizen's defensive plan drove a wedge between Patsy and Rylie which would last well beyond the years to come. They would look like the best of friends in public but when the cameras were off duty and the developed pictures were uploaded on Pinstabook, their true colors would be clearer than glass. At the moment, Patsy was just happy she was getting attention from Kaizen. She knew many ladies would take a bullet just to be in the position she was in during these months. Unfortunately for her, Kaizen was a man of science. And as a man of science, his fancy gravitated to the finer things in life. Such as Radisson Quebec. Radisson, in the eyes of the righteous Kaizen, was just so perfectly fine. What made Radisson so especially alluring to Kaizen, was just how much she wanted to ravage him. All of those days Radisson spent staring outside of her window just to hopefully get a glimpse of Kaizen and all of those nights fantasizing about him, were bound to pay off someday.

Seek PR

February, March and April were filled with lots of back and forth between Kaizen and Patsy. She would find any and every excuse to go over to Bleu Moon while Kaizen would make sure to act coy anytime she was around by always heading directly to his room and locking the door. Not that it was hard for him to act coy, after all, he was not interested in her and he was busy trying to escape the premeditated murderers. But Patsy's fantasies kept her hopes of one day being Kaizen's lover, as well as Kaizen, alive.

The rest of the Bleu Moon boys and girls wanted to end Kaizen once and for all, but many complications came their way. For one, Patsy was so deeply infatuated with Kaizen which made it difficult to truly go through with this act without completely destroying Patsy's desires. Then, there was also all of the coursework that needed to be accomplished by everyone. None of the Bleu Moon boys and girls had really planned ahead in this department. Gair hired a tutor to help her out but it did not help her progress one bit, if anything, it just complicated her life even more. The Bleu Moon boys and girls were just not at the same level of preparedness as Kaizen.

While the Bleu Moon boys and girls were playing catchup and getting distracted with spring break holidays and the annual gatherings in Las Begass via their school network to attend major college basketball events, Kaizen had already found a new home back home. All Kaizen needed to do was charter a private plane to his new apartment to close on his new home and come back to dispose of his personal belongings. Kaizen had closed on his new apartment while everyone else was dilly dallying in the streets of Las Begass during the month of March, trying to find any sort of cheap amusement at every corner that they stumbled upon. During Kaizen's quests to his favorite bookstore this last semester, he had already envisioned how to make the lives of the Bleu Moon boys and girls even more difficult than they already were.

During the two years of housing together with Kaizen, the Bleu Moon boys and girls were not the most courteous of housemates. They would plan events at times they believed would be most bothersome to Kaizen. It wasn't until this last year, when everyone was locked in together due to a mysterious kungflu virus, that they decided to turn up the notch on their level of obnoxiousness. Knowing Kaizen lived directly underneath the main living room, they would find any excuse to turn on the speaker and have little random house dance parties. Fortunately for

Kaizen, he was the most laser focused individual in the world. Their pathetic attempts at distraction didn't bother him as much as they thought it would. But Kaizen took note of their nuisance-filled intentions.

It had not been enough that they played obnoxiously loud music in the living room during every moment of leisure they attained, they had tried to toy with something as sacred and as important as what Patsy felt for Kaizen. Love. At least Patsy was both infatuated and in love with Kaizen, while everyone else had at one point in time during their stay only been merely infatuated by his subdued hunkiness. Such a shame that they had chosen Patsy to be their scapegoat. They knew the astounding level of admiration she had for Kaizen, and using that for their own murderous desires was just pure evil. At least Kaizen would have enough prudence to be gentle when he inevitably added her to the long list of hearts he had broken.

Kaizen ensured that this level of gentle nature was nowhere to be found with the rest of them. In life, the biggest pain any indiviudal could experience is not death, but rather, purgatory in the flesh. Nothing is more damaging to an individual than constantly being looked at by friends, colleagues, acquaintances, and the random stranger that has heard one's stories, with a look of disgust. A disgust that would plague their endeavors, as every door of TRUE opportunity in the form of astounding riches would be shut in their face. This is what awaited the Bleu Moon boys and girls.

In the meantime, during the last month of the school year, Kaizen would ensure that they met their horrible fate in the most obnoxious way possible. Since Kaizen had already found a place to live and he had finished all of his coursework, he had nothing but time. Every moment not on school conference, and every moment he had time to eat his meals, Kaizen would turn up the volume all the way up on his personal speaker. Sometimes he would also go outside into the fresh air to play his speaker, just so that they could get a much needed taste of that protected freedom of speech. During the evenings, right after the Bleu Moon boys and girls had come back to the house from escaping the noise, he would play the same obnoxious song so that their minds would become unfocused and cause them to fall behind on their schoolwork.

They lacked the level of focus Kaizen Domina possessed. They lacked the level of preparedness Kaizen Domina possessed. When they went into their school conferences, they looked as if they had just been possessed. No amount of makeup could hide their haunted faces. No amount of water could revive them enough to perform their beloved day to day tasks. This state

of impotence plagued the Bleu Moon boys and
girls.

Eventually, the Bleu Moon boys and
girls had identified the source of their fatigue. It
was Kaizen's distraction producing speaker. They
could not handle all of those good vibrations.
After all, their bodies were mostly made of water.
These vibrations were bound to drain them of
their energy. But not Kaizen, he was prepared and
in control. By the beginning of May, as
graduation neared, Kaizen had already disposed
of most of his furniture from Bleu Moon. It was
during this time that Chap, Lyon and Gair had
decided that they would throw the dead rat they
had found in the kitchen, into Kaizen's room.
They didn't know who had killed the rat, but they
suspected it had been Kaizen. Good deductive
skills, but not good enough to make a living out of
them. What they were least aware of, was of the
camera Kaizen had placed in his room.
When Gair opened Kaizen's room after knocking
furiously in an attempt to intimidate Kaizen, he
was nowhere to be found. He was in his new
apartment waiting for any notifications of
movement within his room. "Shit head" Gair
thought out loud when she believed Kaizen had
left his room unattended. Gair, after a moment of
analyzing the room, gasped when she met the tiny
eye of the camera Kaizen had strategically placed.
"Wait guys, don't come in. There's a camera. He

knows!" Gair screamed at Lyon and Chap. Lyon, being the dumbass that he is, quickly snuck his head in the room to get a glimpse of what Gair was gasping at, only to catch himself gasping as well, realizing he had been caught on camera. They threw the rat in the basement storage room and fled the scene.

During the course of his stay at Bleu Moon, Kaizen had gathered all sorts of misdeeds performed by the Bleu Moon boys and girls. This was but one of those misdeeds. Granted, this last piece of evidence where Gair and Lyon's gasping faces were caught on camera was indeed the most embarrassing. It was all Kaizen needed in order to give them their very well deserved purgatory in the flesh. He chartered a private plane back to Bleu Moon to clear his belongings from the room and return his keys to the landlord. Kaizen entered and left the house when no one was around and left faster than a speeding bullet. He didn't bother to give Gair rent that last month. They didn't deserve his rent money and besides, Kaizen had been the one providing everyone with free internet service. They had nothing to complain about. During the graduation ceremony taking place on the ninth May day of the year Two Thousand & Twenty-One, Kaizen was nowhere to be found in the graduating crowd. His diploma was already on the way to his postal box. That day, in his new apartment, he took the time to disconnect all of his connections on his Pinstabook, but not before uploading a temporary short video exposing all of Bleu Moon's misdeeds. His short but significant list of followers were now made aware of the true scum going by the names of Lyon Measle, Chap Chamberlin, Fagan Fogarty, Gair Mallard, Yerma McCallum and Ruth Leslie Lyon. The only way they had a chance of surviving this social shit storm and resuscitating their reputation, was if they were able to attract the help of a Public Relations firm. Unfortunately, none of them could afford such help. Too bad. So sad.

"And that's the way it is."

After graduation, following Kaizen's extravagant exposé, Lyon fled back to his parents' home. The other Bleu Moon boys and girls had done the same. Becker & Carey Measle's humble abode was located at 5421 W Heartford Ave #5421, Sterile Valley, Copperdition 32803. Copperdition was about one state southeast from another state known as Cuencarda. Given Lyon's pathetic financial situation, he had no other housing options. For someone who was a son to a 'man' within the real estate industry, one would think that Lyon would know by now how to find a much better place to set his nest. Anywhere was better than that godless hellhole of a state going by copperdition, especially if the only option was going back home to room with one's parents.

Lyon pretended like going back home to live with his parents didn't bother him. He pretended like it was okay to not have the know-how in getting his own apartment. He truly exceled at pretending. But even with such pretentious skills, it was difficult for him to pretend like he was a better man than Kaizen. Lyon was a boy trapped in the body of a young man. Lyon became extremely depressed when word got around that Kaizen ended up landing an apartment in one of the most prolific and wealthiest parts of the nation while he was still in a shitty shithole in Copperdition. *At least I have graduate school to look forward to*, he thought.

Lyon spent all summer contemplating the many routes he could take in life that would help him somehow be seen as a victim of Kaizen. He just had to figure out how he could do it tactfully, he didn't want to draw too much attention to Kaizen or otherwise, everyone would truly know just how much of a pathetic loser Lyon actually was. Lyon schemed and schemed. Finally, he thought it would be a good idea to make a website that would showcase his own media company. He thought it would be a great idea to focus on videography within the sports industry, as if there was any profit in that. No one looked more delusional than Lyon when he just ended up getting a subordinate job for a Copperdition's basketball team, which happened to be within the world's most highly esteemed basketball league. He thought that showcasing individuals that were barely household names, within those houses unfortunate enough to follow something as futile as basketball of course, would somehow help him propel his career. It didn't. It just ended up making him look like one of the biggest pretentious idiots the world had encountered. He would never amount to anything as great as Kaizen.

Lyon had always been plagued with delusions of grandeur. He believed that the more connections he possessed, the more important he was. He even believed that he was more important than those connections he thought made him important. This thought process never did him well. It didn't do him well during The Hawt Seat game when he pretended to be buddies with Kaizen. It didn't do him well when his false sense of self-importance was prevalent during Gair Mallard's birthday party, as every attendee was disgusted by it. He even believed that his fake ex-girlfriend, who helped him live in the closet for as long as he wanted, should not be seen with Kaizen as it would undermine Lyon's very own fake masculinity. Lyon believed it was no big deal using Kaizen's well earned money to indulge himself in nonsensical pleasures. That is the level of importance Lyon believed he had.

He believed he was intelligent and above all. Especially Kaizen. This hubris had prevailed even after his failed attempt to kill off Kaizen. It even prevailed when his true colors had been exposed to the gatekeepers of the riches of the world via Kaizen's Pinstabook. Lyon being Lyon, was still in denial of this and pretended to go through his sad career and graduate years like he was the salt of the earth.

The most influential newscaster of all time known as Malter Arkwright, may he rest in peace, would not approve of a vermin like Lyon. Malter Arkwright held a habit of virtue through his authentic reporting and ability to tell the truth. These were virtuous traits and habits that Lyon never held and would never be able to grasp even after graduate school. The most ironic thing about Lyon's journalistic aspirations, which he gave up on as soon as he made a low tier website to unsuccessfully spite Kaizen, is that Lyon went on to attend the journalism program that Malter Arkwright himself helped establish. This journalism program weakened with Lyon's attendance.

However, Lyon believed this journalism program would engorge his delusions of grandeur disguised as self-importance even more. It was another accolade that could be used to make himself believe he was worthy of living. It was not enough. Kaizen's success after college cast a shadow on these childish trophies. Kaizen was making his clients millions of dollars with his copywriting abilities while Lyon was still formulating what other skills he should showcase on his cheap website. So Lyon listed off some more labels on his website... Videographer... Editor... Writer... Reporter. These were the best run of the mill buzz words Lyon could come up with in hopes of aggrandizing himself even more.

It did nothing tangible for him. This was because, well, nobody really cared what Lyon thought of himself. They could tell right away he was full of crap. But at least, he thought, he could use it in his pathetic stories. Stories where he could victimize himself, yet, seem like a true mass media genius. *Oh, there was this man whom I used to dorm with and he totally copied my style. He totally wants to be me. He wishes he was me...* is the story he thought he could tell to get others to think highly of him. Nobody ever would. His hubris kept him like a blind mouse for the rest of his life. Even the biggest dimwit would never want to be behind a camera capturing moving pictures of men dribbling a ball only to post it on ClickClock with no trackable margin of profit. This same dimwit would also have enough common sense to pity the fool living such a Sisyphus like existence.

That is the way it always was. That is the way it will continue to be. And that's the way it is.

Last Begass

Ever since their March get together in Las Begass, Cuencarda during their last semester being pupils at Gorgonzola College, the Bleu Moon boys and girls had made it a habit to get together in similar fashion for years to come. Year after year, they would get together in Las Begass as they felt they fit right and could be themselves. They believed that what happens in Las Begass, stays in Las Begass. This location would serve as a point of reconnection for them, and to pretend like their College misdeeds had been a thing of the past. The Bleu Moon boys and girls began to fill up with just as much hubris as Lyon had always held during his college years.

During that first reunion, occuring a year after graduation, the Bleu Moon boys and girls could not find any feasible way to make their criminal scandal go away. Most of the people that knew them from college would murmur, quite loudly, as they neared their presence. Those murmurs questioned their rumored criminal activities during college. *Had they really locked Kaizen in and out of the house? Did they really try to kill Kaizen as he claims they did? If so, why is Kaizen still alive?* These were all questions that floated the venues in which the Bleu Moon boys and girls attended. They did their best to ignore it. But these glares and comments always gnawed at them every time they reunited at Las Begass.

The Bleu Moon boys and girls could've chosen to not keep coming back to Las Begass. But they did not stop going to Las Begass for quite a few years. They believed that the more they went there to pass time and pretend like they were free of any wrongdoings, the more people would believe them to be incapable of harming someone like Kaizen. And they would've gone away with it too, if most of the people in the world lacked as much common sense as they did. EVERYONE knew the true pieces of shit that they were. As such, they just merely let them slowly burn themselves in that hot desert that fills Cuencarda. Everyone knew they were not worth the judiciary hassle. After all, it was a free country, and true pieces of shit are free to burn themselves in the sun if they so desire. It was just another manifestation of attempts at escaping the shitty reality of their lives.

When the Bleu Moon boys and girls believed that they fit right into Las Begass, Cuencarda... they were not wrong. It is a place filled with very few intelligent life forms. The entirety of the services offered at Las Begass cater to the most primitive desires. There is nothing wrong with services fulfilling the most primitive desires of mankind, but the manner in which it is exhibited in Cuencarda is extremely unbecoming. Only those who have most in common with neanderthals would find this place appealing. It was as if they were not aware of the modern digital realm. There was no taste to the exhibition of the services offered at Las Begass. Every direction one could turn to, there were tacky attempts at elegance. This became more evident to the Bleu Moon boys and girls the more they reunited as the years went by.

As time went by, the Bleu Moon boys and girls seemed to become more and more possessed by depression. This was because they could not escape the stories about Kaizen and the billions of dollars in revenue he was generating via his well oiled advertising agency. It was unbelievable. Kaizen was not someone that became well known to the masses throughout his lifetime, yet, his presence was known by an elite few that were responsible of shaping the world. These elite few would ensure to never make the Bleu Moon boys and girls a part of their ecosystem, as it would cause atrophy in the quest of bettering mankind. The Bleu Moon boys suspected this was the case. It was only Lyon that seemed to have this certainty of damnation within his life.

As the reunions stacked with the years to come, Lyon's mind became stacked with more and more negative thoughts. He became possessed by them. During his last reunion with the Bleu Moon boys and girls, he didn't seem quite like himself. He seemed dazed and confused. During this last reunion, he had called it a night very early in the young night, and returned back to the private residence he had booked for his stay at Las Begass. On the way over to the private residence, Lyon remembered all the work he had done for the Bleu Moon boys and girls, yet, they never convinced Fagan to sodomize him. As soon as he had arrived at the residence, he took out the cardboard covered wide-ruled composition notebook he always carried with him as well as the calligraphy pen he had used to write all of the thoughts that filled his head. Tonight's thoughts seemed a little different. They didn't have the same inquisitive structure that he always seemed to use, and instead, had a rather poetically charged structure to it. After finishing putting his thoughts on paper, he took off the entirety of his bottom wear until he was half naked. With his calligraphy pen, he drew three very congruent circles on the floor. He had essentially made a venn diagram, to which he placed a finishing touch by adding another congruent circle right in the middle which would create a triquetra figure within the entirety of the figure.

Lyon then placed his notebook on top of the triquetra where he could read it, and continued to lay his pelvis on the floor where he had made the triquetra, still with pen in hand. He used his left hand to keep his notebook open during his calligraphy session, and kept it open when he chanted what he had calligraphed. During the entirety of his chant, Lyon drew many similar figures to the one he had drawn on the floor on both of his hamstrings in miniature form. Without looking. It was as if he was possessed by a higher being.

Who hath possessed Lyon Measle, one shall never know.
What his evil deeds have impacted, is more than one shall know.
Where the rippling waters go, cast a stone and truth you'll know.
When the Lady's moon is new, kiss the hand to her, times two.
When the moon rides at her peak, then your hearts desire seek.
When the wind comes from the South, love will kiss thee on the mouth.
When the wind blows from the West, departed souls will have no rest.
When the wind blows from the East, expect the new and set the feast.
When the Wheel begins to turn, let the Beltane fires burn.

*When the Wheel has turned to Yule, light the log and
the Horned One rules.*
Why if ye harm none, then ye shall do what ye will.
Mind the Threefold Law, is what ye forgot to do.
Three times bad and three times good.
It comes back times three!

Lyon subsequently sucked his right
thumb and used it to quickly lubricate his rectum
area. From there, Lyon flung his right arm into
the air, and then, with an immense acceleration,
pegged the pen it contained into his anus. He let
out a low-pitched pleasure-filled grunt. Once
more, he flung his right arm into the air and
chanted...

It comes back times three!

With an immense acceleration, Lyon
pegged the pen he contained in his right hand
back into his anus. He let out another low-pitched
pleasure-filled grunt. Once more, he flung his
right arm into the air, except this time he allowed
himself to let out a euphoric sigh before
chanting...

It comes back times three!

With an immense acceleration, Lyon
pegged the pen he contained in his right hand

back into his anus and let out his final low-pitched pleasure-filled grunt. It could now be said that during his Last Begass trip, Lyon had signed his own death warrant. With black ink.

The private residence host eventually found Lyon's body. His death made some news headlines. Lyon's parents were now relieved from such a huge responsibility. Most important of all... balance had now successfully been restored within the universe.

Deadline

By now, enough time had passed for Lyon's horrific tragedy to be seen as a distant memory. A distant yet dense memory. A story that goes around dinner time with participants making recollecting statements such as "Ah yes I remember that sad sap of a story" or "Such a poor soul" and even "What a fucking loser" by the least compassionate. His ridiculous death almost came to be a legend, of the notorious kind of course. Lyon's story was one to be found by those occasionally perusing the news flash section of their favorite press association. His story was nothing but the equivalent of what a face on a milk carton would be today. A dismissed tragedy. Something that got in the way of people living their day to day lives. A disregarded picture.

Such a cautionary tale of incompetence could not be left to waste. Someone like Lyon who was deemed by the random passerby to have all the potential in the world, to turn out to be the biggest waste of air, could make nothing less than an intriguing story to those riding the highest vibrations the world has to offer. There was one huge complication when it came to bringing about this story to life. Not one member, aside from Kaizen Domina, was competent or virtuous enough to bring about such a tale in writing form. It would be a godly task for any mere mortal to successfully complete such a task. For Kaizen, this would be nothing but a mere item in his to-do list.

Lyon's horrific story had two possible outcomes. It could either die off for no one to remember or be immortalized by the person he had despised the most during his time on earth. Either way, Lyon was already dead. Kaizen took this task of writing about Lyon's tragic story very seriously. Sure, nowadays he was busy with much more important matters than writing a story about a simple lying weasel, but he had already been invested with the title of the book. It was something simple. Yet true and effective. The book, if written by Kaizen, would be called "The Lying Weasel". To make the story extra mysterious, he would write it under a pen name which could only be traced back to him by those foolish enough to connect the dots. Kaizen thought "León Adivino" would be a cool sounding pen name. A name that Lyon would have never been able to live up to, even if the pussy had nine lifetimes. It was indeed a lauded name. Many people would soon share the same sentiment about this pseudonym. So clearly, Kaizen's biggest obstacle was not figuring out how to sell the book, or figuring out what to name it, or formulating the blurb. For christ's sake, he had built the highest performing advertising agency in the world during his formative college years! His biggest obstacle to writing this book was the concept of deadline.

It seems as if there are deadlines everywhere and in everything. There is a deadline to a day, and a natural sleeping cycle that comes along with it. Something that was not respected by the Bleu Moon boys and girls after playing The Hawt Seat game. This disrespect became a habit to them. Their bodies would accumulate the toll as time went by. Even celebrations have deadlines, such as the one set by the boys in blue during Gair Mallard's birthday party. Relationships can have deadlines, and most do. Our health and wellbeing requires us to have fasting deadlines, otherwise, there would be no time for breakfast. Aspirations have deadlines, otherwise, we would turn blue at not allowing room for respiration to occur. Fraudulent airs and heirs have deadlines, sooner or later, someone is bound to figure out why the funny smell won't go away.

Intelligently plotted schemes have deadlines. Well designed gas lighting and games have deadlines, after all, the match can only last so long. Trust, Love, Reputation, and LIFE... can all have a deadline. It was this last deadline, the deadline of life, Kaizen was most concerned with. Lyon's death, though ridiculously deserved, reminded Kaizen just how fragile life can be in its end as much as it is in its beginning. Lyon's life had taken up more space than it was worth, and his death had just made more room for something greater to flourish in the world. Kaizen would not let such a blissful void go to waste.

For the greater good of the world, Kaizen would ensure that his next generation would never turn out to be as pathetic as Lyon Measle. This determination was prevalent in all of his work. This evident determination displayed through his career would soon bring about a somewhat familiar face back into his life. Radisson Quebec. She would become tired of admiring Kaizen from afar, and eventually, make contact with Kaizen. Her motivation stemmed from many moments of reminiscing about all that time spent staring at him whenever he would go to read on the backyard bench while they were in college. She was just as sure then, as she is now, that Kaizen was not just another hunky man mindlessly wandering the earth. He was a man constantly on his mission.

Most times, Radisson would be this mission. Other times, another mission would keep him occupied. But for the most part, Kaizen did his best in making Radisson part of as many missions as humanly possible. They were eventually able to fulfill many successful missions together. Six, to be exact. They were all completed before Radisson had reached her fertility deadline. These six successful missions brought about six amazing beings into the world. Each of these beings would turn out to be pretty much like their father. They would be six wittle entrepreneurs. Until they no longer were, and instead, had turned into gigantic business magnates. Just like their father.

Radisson and Kaizen's first creation would immerse itself in the textiles industry. Their second creation would immerse itself in the metals industry. Their third creation would immerse itself in the mineralogical industry. Their fourth creation would immerse itself in the synthetic fibers industry. Their fifth child would immerse itself in the essential oils industry. Their sixth creation, which would come to be Kaizen's favorite child, would immerse itself in the publishing industry. Their last child was Kaizen's favorite because he had been so much more emotionally invested during this creation process than he had been with the previous ones.

After their fifth child together, Radisson could not quite walk as well as she used to. Yet, she insisted on having a sixth child. Kaizen was hesitant as he wasn't sure if she could truly handle more of his precious seed. She was healthy and still owned the same blazing hot physique she had embodied for the last decade.

During these indecisive moments, in a small patch of land within the two million acres of land Kaizen owned, he had built Radisson and the children a modest home. It was in this new home that their last child was conceived. It was in this home where Radisson returned from her last childbirth visit to the hospital. In a wheelchair. Her beauty never disappeared, even in such invalid conditions. Her life force, however, did disappear soon after giving birth to their last child. Kaizen and their children had returned back home from a visit to the park only to find that their home had burned down, with Radisson still inside of it. The firefighters informed Kaizen that they were not able to reach their home with enough time to rescue her fiery soul.

Though Radisson's death made a huge dent in Kaizen's universe, he and his children would ensure her legacy lived on. Aside from being very successful entrepreneurs, Kaizen and Radisson's children would all turn out to be impeccable writers that would fill the world with their vibrant culture. After Kaizen finally joined Radisson in the afterlife, their children had all made their own imprint within the publishing company owned by Radisson and Kaizen's sixth child. Each imprint was immensely successful in their own unique regard.

The End.

As Above, So Below.

As Within, So Without.

As The Universe, So The Soul.

Bwahahahahahaha!!

Hahahahaha!

Ha.

www.ingramcontent.com/pod-product-compliance
Lightning Source LLC
Chambersburg PA
CBHW050851180626
46814CB00007B/2726